HELLGOING

HELLGOING

STORIES

LYNN COADY

This edition published in 2013 by
House of Anansi Press Inc.
110 Spadina Avenue, Suite 801
Toronto, ON, M5V 2K4
Tel. 416-363-4343
Fax 416-363-1017
www.houseofanansi.com

Distributed in Canada by
HarperCollins Canada Ltd.
1995 Markham Road
Scarborough, ON, M1B 5M8
Toll free tel. 1-800-387-0117

17 16 15 14 13   2 3 4 5 6

Library and Archives Canada Cataloguing in Publication

Coady, Lynn, 1970–, author
Hellgoing : stories / Lynn Coady.

Issued in print and electronic formats.
ISBN 978-1-77089-308-5 (pbk.).—ISBN 978-1-77089-309-2 (html)

I. Title.

PS8555.O23H44 2013   C813'.54   C2013-902745-9
                        C2013-902746-7

Cover design: Alysia Shewchuk
Text design and typesetting: Alysia Shewchuk

 Canada Council   Conseil des Arts
for the Arts   du Canada

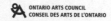 ONTARIO ARTS COUNCIL
CONSEIL DES ARTS DE L'ONTARIO

*We acknowledge for their financial support of our publishing program
the Canada Council for the Arts, the Ontario Arts Council, and the Government of Canada
through the Canada Book Fund.*

Printed and bound in Canada

For Rob

For, though I've no idea
What this accoutred frowsty barn is worth,
It pleases me to stand in silence here
— Philip Larkin

CONTENTS

WIRELESS

WIRELESS

Jane salutes you from an age where to be an aficionado is to find yourself foolishly situated in the world. Where to care a great deal about something, no matter how implicitly interesting it may be, is to come across as a kind of freak. It's interest—inordinate interest—in something seemingly arbitrary, having little to do with you or the context you inhabit. Beanie Babies, say, or Glenn Gould. Jane once met a person who insisted he was "crazy about Glenn Gould," who owned all these rare and exotic recordings. Called himself a glennerd, happily, smugly. Did other Gould fanatics call themselves glennerds? Jane wanted to know. The glennerd shrugged, didn't care. It wasn't about other glennerds, Jane saw, it was only about this particular glennerd, him and his fascination. This person was not a musician. Didn't listen to classical music, as a rule.

It's that people get fixated. People take a notion in their head. Jane, not her real name because all this embarrasses her somewhat, once had a thing for a cartoon called *Robo-friendz*. She was too old for *Robo-friendz* — sixteen, she was supposed have things for men with tawny chests, bulging crotches and leonine hair — but no, only the Robo-friendz, for about a year or so, sent her into a daily couch-catatonia. No one in her family was allowed to talk to her when *Robo-friendz* was on. She probably drooled as she watched, as slackly comforted — comfortably absented — as a baby nuzzling breasts. These are the obsessions that turn your brain somehow on and off at once. They come regularly, each more arbitrary than the next. Once it was mushrooms, especially the kind that look like tiny, mounted brains. Once it was an all-male medieval choir from Norway. Once it was a website with a dancing hamster who sang a different show tune every week. She checked it faithfully each Monday morning, like a prayer to greet the dawn. It is not like alcoholism, it is not like addiction. But it's wrapped up with that — the pathetic psychology of it. The everlasting need to flee whatever there is to be fled from. Fortunately, one does not need to dwell on this knowledge, one is discouraged from beating oneself up in Jane's circles. That's good to know — you're permitted to comprehend and yet ignore such things — that's nice, that helps.

IT STARTED BEFORE the dream. A woman walks into a bar. Starts like a joke, you see.

A woman walks into a bar. It's Toronto, she's there on business. Bidness, she likes to call it, she says to her friends. Makes it sound raunchy, which it is not. It's meetings, mostly with other women of her own age or else men about twenty years older. Sumptuous lunches in blandly posh restaurants. There is only one thing duller than upscale Toronto dining, and that's upscale Toronto dining with women of Jane's own age, class and education. They and Jane wear black, don't go in for a lot of jewellery, are elegant, serious. The men are more interesting. The men were once Young Turks of publishing. They remember the seventies, when magazines were run by young men exactly like themselves—smokers, drinkers—and these men have never found one another remotely dull—not in the least. Some of them used to be in rock and roll bands. They wear their hair a little shaggy around the ears, now, a silvery homage. Some of them have even managed to remain drunks. This is something a lady discovers quickly over lunch: which of these silver foxes are recovered, and which are still sloshing around down there in the dregs. Wine with lunch, Jane? Oh well, perhaps I'll join you. Half litre? Heck, why not a full one, how often do you get into town? Martini to round out dessert? Specialty coffee? At this point, both sets of eyes are liquid, glinting friendly light.

If it doesn't happen at lunch, she'll go to a bar, later in the day, after dinner. She has a sense of decorum. She can wait until after dinner, especially when she's on Vancouver time, three hours earlier than this grey, weighty city.

So a woman walks into a bar. Meets a man—it's a cliché. The man is also a drunk, also an out-of-towner, also alone. After the first round, they are delighted to discover they come from precisely opposite sides of the continent. Oh, ho ho ho. Delighted in that dumb, convivial way that drinking people have. It's not like it can be considered a coincidence, being from opposite sides of the country. But, oh, ho ho ho, they find it an inexplicable delight. To be meeting up right here in the middle.

His accent was a giveaway from the start. His quaint, alien accent, the way he can't pronounce *th*, it's twee, she finds it cute. You're not supposed to find Newfoundlanders cute, they bristle at that. Some people are the same way about Newfoundlanders as others are about Beanie Babies and Glenn Gould. But his name is Ned, he's burly, has a beard and is a fiddler. I mean, come on.

In town to play some bars with his five-part folk/trad outfit. They specialize in filthy songs, he tells her, dirty ditties. Smutty traditional tunes from days gone by, baroque with double — and sometimes single — entendres. Most people don't want to know that cute Newfoundlanders and their Irish antecedents went around singing things like: *Come and tie my pecker round a tree, round a tree-o / come and tie my tool around a tree.* But, says Ned, they did, and do. Ned bears himself up like a scholar as he tells her this. As the evening unspools, he sings snatches from his repertoire, and indeed most of it has to do with snatches in some way or another. The only one she is able to remember afterward is a song that kept ending with the refrain "bangin' on the ol' tin can."

"I never heard it called that before."

"We are a colourful people," Ned had agreed.

Ned wanted to go home with her — to her hotel and not his, because he was sharing his room with the accordion player. But when that idea was vetoed by the unenticed Jane—he was too burly, too bearded for her sleek tastes— he recommended they at least keep in touch. So she took his phone and email.

"If you're ever on the Rock," he'd offered with bourboned sincerity.

THE DREAM CAME after, months and months after, and had nothing to do with Ned, even if Ned was the first thing she thought of once she was able to think, that morning.

You have hangover dreams. They usually involve drinking. Not booze; water, because you're so dehydrated it's all your mind can think about. And on some level of sleep awareness, you know you are in tremendous pain, so you dream about relief. A cold compress administered to your head by an infinitely gentle nurse, an angel straight out of Hemingway. All white but for the roses in her cheeks. You dream of tender mercies and cool pale hands extending long drinks of water. A tumbler from the freezer—a delicate glaze of ice floating on top, frost fuzzing the sides. Wildly vivid—your mind's so thirsty. It paints the most alluring picture it can.

That's what Jane's mind was engaged in this one morning. In all its desperation, it cobbled together the most beautiful dream she's ever had. Floating on her back in the ocean, icebergs all around. *Cool, clear water*, a voice was singing distantly. It sounded like Tennessee Ernie Ford. Everything blue and white—crystalline. The icebergs loomed gigantically, sheltering her. The sun was somewhere, but hidden. It was bright, but not dazzling. She wasn't cold, floating there in the frozen ocean. She was cool.

Cool, clear water, affirmed Tennessee Ernie. Then she woke up.

She lay flat on her back for twenty minutes, gauging the pain, the depth of her dehydration. The song in her ears. She sat up, and a second later her pickled brain slid back into its cradle in the centre of her cranium. Time to throw up.

Afterward, fumbling nearly an entire tray of ice cubes into a martini shaker and dumping tap water up to the brim, she went to her computer. Brought up Google Images and spent the next three hours with them.

This was on Sunday, the day of rest. Nonetheless, she allowed herself a quick bidness email. Dean, one of the Toronto silver foxes. Reformed. Now Dean is all about yoga — having developed one of those ropy, male yoga bodies, flexible to the point of the grotesque. Nicely recovered from the seventies bacchanals, when he had run a small poetry press out of his bedroom, getting sloppy punches thrown at him by Milton Acorn, sleeping with Leonard Cohen's braless castoffs. Dean now oversees an in-flight magazine.

Hiya Dean, she wrote. I'm thinking of doing a travel piece.

It took three more emails, including an elaborate two-page pitch plus one wheedling phone call to get Dean to agree to pay expenses. Her ace in the hole was the Hollywood movie, blessedly just released. Badly rendered on the whole, but beautifully shot, a veritable travelogue. Tourists were flocking as a result—flocking! she told Dean. She'd cribbed this from her conversation with Ned, who gave her to understand in no uncertain terms that any Newfoundlander worth his salt would wince like foot-meets-jellyfish at mention of the movie. Would bemoan the clothes ("Nobody dresses like that!"), the accents ("like a retarded Blanche DuBois"), the incest ("always with the goddamn incest"). Plus the actors, reportedly, had put on airs. And Ned's brother had been hired for use of his boat and the bastards had hauled stakes for L.A. still owing him money.

None of this made it into the three emails and one phone call with Dean. Just the movie, and the tourists, buying up the books, sweaters, CDs and partridgeberry jam like it was going out of style, which of course it was.

Was it ever in style to be a lady drunk, she'd wondered, back when she was nearing her thirtieth birthday and becoming recognizable to herself. From reading, Jane determined it was not. Good for Jane, therefore: iconoclast. She calls herself Jane in a roundabout homage to her heroine, the alcoholic novelist Jean Rhys. Jane didn't like the name, however, the pinched sound of it —Jeen Rees— like eye-slits. Jean had been a terrible alcoholic. Which is to say, she was bad at it. Jane, on the other hand, is an impeccable drunk in her driven, Type A sort of way. Jean floundered about the streets of London and Paris, roaring up at Ford Madox Ford's window, threatening her landladies, getting arrested. Men used her and she used them in return, but never managed to derive the same blithe satisfaction from it. She let herself get beaten down, let herself get poor and old and conspicuously smashed. Flattened into *Jeen*.

SHE SEES FROM the plane. Big clumps of wedding cake floating on the deep and endless blue. Reverse sky, jagged clouds.

"Oh, look, there they are!" she says to the seatmate she has ignored for the entire jaunt from Halifax. But doesn't turn away to see if he is looking too. Now she can see the roots of them beneath the water, extending to who-knows-what depths. Of course, the bulk of these monoliths remains underwater. Hence the old "tip of the iceberg" saying. To mean: This is just the beginning. You think this is something? This is *nothing*.

JANE FLOPS HERSELF off Ned like a seal, grunting also like a seal. That's what she feels like at such times. All torso, no limbs. A long, tapering creature, new and primordial, like something pooped out of something else.

All night since they met up at the bar it had been: Not gonna sleep with Ned, Not gonna sleep with Ned, until around one-forty-five in the morning when she decided, Ah why not. Now it is nine hours later, and Ned stayed the night either because he is a gent or because it's a nice hotel room. She is staying at the Delta. Ned had invited her to stay at his place, had insisted, had been appalled she would turn down a stranger's pullout couch for a clean, well-lighted place with a sweeping view of the downtown and harbour beyond. Ned had that down-home hospitality beaten into him along with the holy catechism, she assumed.

He'd told her about that sort of stuff, once they were properly liquored. Catholic school. A teacher taking him aside and punching him in the stomach when he was eight.

"That'll learn ya," Jane had smirked, looking down.

"It did learn me," said Ned, brown-eyed and serious above his beard.

Jane wiped the smirk off her face.

"What did it learn you?" she wanted to know, being serious herself now, if not quite enough to correct her syntax.

"Fear," answered Ned. "That's what school's for. To teach us to be afraid, right?"

"That's what *everything's* for."

Oh it is horseshit that drunkards don't have real conversations, don't connect with others on any kind of significant level. Jane once had a boyfriend who joined AA just to shame her, because she wouldn't go and he thought she needed to. Then he would come home and tell her everything he'd learned at that evening's meetings. The thing that hurt her feelings the most was when he told her there was no point having a conversation with a drunk. Nothing they said was real, he informed her, nothing they could say had any depth or meaning. They could declare their undying love for you at night and forget they had uttered a word of it in the morning.

She looks over at Ned. Perhaps there have been little to no beautiful moments shared between them thus far, but

Ned has told her a story that's rubbed at her heart, brought her to the point of *Ah why not*, caused her to say something she would normally be far too slick to utter, to practically yelp it, eyes bulging, turning nearby heads.

"That's what *everything's* for."

Almost giving away the farm.

JEAN RHYS WAS always cold in England. Thus it is with Jane, who brought precisely the wrong kind of clothes for Newfoundland. It is May, which apparently is not quite springtime around here. She neglected to pack hats or gloves or scarves. Her ears glow the moment she steps outside. It's a good wind.

Jean Rhys used to cuddle up under blankets in her own hotel and boarding house rooms — as many blankets as she could — placing an arm over her eyes (she mentions this gesture in several stories, the supine, defeated woman on the bed, arm over the eyes). Then Jean would drift into dreams of her island home, Dominica — imagine herself growing moist and sultry from the tropical sun, not the heat of her body under thick woolen blankets. At one place, she took hot baths so often the landlady made remarks about it. Indecent implications. What kind of girl, she would ask in front of all the other boarders, took so many hot baths?

And what did Jean say? How did Jean react to this indignity? Jean said nothing. Jean went upstairs, lay down. Covered her eyes with her arm. Let the cold settle into her bones like rot.

SHE AND NED are hiking Signal Hill. Ned is disinclined, keeps wanting to sit on a bench and smoke. Ned is a constant surprise to her—she'd thought the beard a sort of Grizzly Adams-ish indicator of his island-man's love of the outdoors.

"Ned," says Jane. She stretches her hamstrings on the bench while he struggles to light his cigarette in the wind. "You've got to take better care of yourself. It's our responsibility as drunks to look after ourselves, make sure we eat right and get regular exercise and all that, because the bastards are just looking for any excuse to tell you how irresponsible you are, how you're ruining your health, how you're a drain on society. It's up to us to throw it all back in their faces, to say, What are you talking about, look at me, I'm fine. I earn money. I pay my rent or my mortgage or whatever. I have friends, I'm successful in what I do. Who are you to judge me, and on what possible basis?"

Ned's not saying anything. She looks over. He's still got the cigarette between his lips, the lighter poised, his hands cupped against the wind. But he's no longer flicking away.

"What?" she says.

"Who're you calling a drunk?" says Ned.

"Denial," she lectures, "is even worse. Denial gives them all the ammunition they could possibly need. Allows for feelings of superiority. Don't give them the satisfaction, Ned."

Ned stands, gestures at the bald rock on every side— smoke in one hand, lighter in the other. "Who's them?" He says. "Where they all at?"

"Everyone," she insists, flapping her hands in the wind.

A particularly violent gust rocks her, for a moment, takes Ned's smoke. He doesn't bother to chase it.

She wishes he would go because she'd like to be by herself when she first sees them. Once she and Ned clear the bend, beyond the harbour, the bergs stand in full view, dazzling white against two different, dazzling shades of blue. She wonders which whimsical, goofball description will work best for the article. *We rounded the bend and experienced our first breathtaking view. Like massive clouds had hardened in the heavens and fallen to the sea.* Awful. Jane's mind keeps lingering on the tooth analogy — but what kind of description would that make? *Like really, really big teeth.*

Then she realizes why she's having so much trouble. It's blasphemy, what she's doing — her deep-mind is rebelling. She has almost fooled herself, along with everyone else, into believing the article is what she's here for. She doesn't want to describe them, it would be wrong to describe them. She won't do it. This is part of the self-control she was advocating to Ned only a moment ago. Who's them? asks Ned. Them as in: Never let them see you sweat. Never let them see you drunk. Never let them know you look at icebergs.

She jogs a bit ahead on the narrow path. Ned calling, "Don't fall!" as she disappears behind a dip of rock. Stands by herself gazing seaward for the time it takes him to catch up. "Jeez, Ned," she says when he does, pretending to have been bored, unoccupied.

They get to the top after an hour of this. Ned has no interest in going into the tower and neither does Jane, but she supposes she has to in order to make obligatory mention of it in the article.

"Nah," says Ned. "It's just a gift shop and stuff about Marconi." Jane has wandered over to the pay-telescope or whatever it's called as Ned settles on a bench and lights his fourth smoke of the hike. She digs around in her pack for a dollar. "Of course, you'll get a better view from the tower," he remarks before she can place it in the slot.

"Oh. There's a scope up there?"

"Up the top," he says. "You can see the gulls landing on the bergs."

"You know what," remembers Jane, "I didn't even think to buy souvenirs yet."

"Do you need any money?" he calls as she darts away. The man is one exotic bird.

Marconi is a serene-looking man, sitting in front of his wire-thing—it really is just a bundle of wires, wires for a so-called "wireless" transmission. He's in a desolate room but a dapper hat and suit, dressed for the occasion, to change the world. Head turned slightly to glance at the camera as if to say, *Oh, this? No big deal.* She tries to read about him and his world-changing wire-thing. Marconi, she notes, was an "amateur" in the burgeoning world of radio communication at the turn of the last century. Of course. He was like Jane, like the glennerd, an aficionado, only with more commitment, consistency and breadth of vision. Marconi wouldn't have wasted his time on *Robofriendz.* But Jane is certain he was after the same sort of thing, up here with his bundle of wire and big crazy kite in the middle of December. The single-mindedness is what's key, the tunnel vision—precisely what's required and precisely what makes you seem a freak to the rest of the world. Visionaries and drinkers: obsessed with away, looking for *else*.

Something to guard against, though, Jane reminds herself. Classic drunkard mentality. That appalling self-absorption—relating everything back to one's own experience, no matter how trifling one's own experience might be. Marconi? Oh, yeah, he's just like me. And icebergs are my thing, by the way, I'm the only one in the world who's ever been interested in icebergs. She recalls a humiliatingly defining moment in a restaurant, visiting with a long-lost friend to whom she'd always felt a pinch inferior. She'd been so deep into her own navel the entire time that, as the friend detailed the difficulties of married life, Jane had finally glared across the table and spoke. "I guess I'm not like you. I'm not looking to settle down." She'd said it in a strained, defensive way, as if the woman across the table had been sitting there smirking at her, lording her wifely status. But then Jane noticed her old friend's face, registered her sadness and then her astonishment, followed by an ironic sort of wilt to the shoulders. The blood roared into Jane's ears and cheeks as the sheer, breathless scale of her mistake sunk in. The friend rested her face on an open hand, weary. She spoke Jane's name as if calling from a distance. "I'm telling you my relationship is falling apart," she said, leaning toward Jane. "We're splitting up. It's hard for me."

Rhys, too, had the drinker's megalomania. Jean thought everyone was out to get her, men in particular. She even spent her spare time writing elaborate fictional court transcripts, fashioning herself as the eternal defendant. But it wasn't that men were out to get her. They just had no idea about this woman—a woman of the world, of Paris cafés and London dance halls, a married and divorced woman, a woman who lived through two world wars and had two husbands arrested and jailed. What kind of woman emerges at the end of all this with an emotional skin like the membrane between shell and egg? You couldn't blame the men—they didn't want to hurt Jean. But who could have fathomed a creature so hurtable?

AT FOUR IN the morning, a man out on the street is banging on somebody's door. St. John's is a shockingly quiet place at night, like the middle of the woods. Except for this man, a drunk of course, banging on somebody's door on the street below. He exists, thinks Jane, like an avatar of her mind, a golem shaped from the muck of her obsessions. The Bad Drunk. The creature Jane will never be.

He's yelling someone's name, it sounds like *Ray!* or *Jay!* A long *a* sound—maybe even just *Hey!* He'll hammer a good ten or so hammers, machine-gun quick on Ray or Jay's screen door before screaming out Ray or Jay's name. No inkling that Ray or Jay may not be inclined to open his door to a raging drunk at four in the morning. Drunks— as innocent as lambs sometimes. *We can't afford it*, Jane wants to holler down at him.

Now the lone car starts up on the other side of town. Someone has called the cops. She grins to herself, lying there, listening to the car meander its way through the streets. No element of surprise at work here. They might as well just call to the crooks across town—from the Tim Hortons or wherever—*Yeah, we hear you; now just stay put.* He hears them too—the desperate man in the street. The door-banging stops all at once. Seconds before the cop car arrives. Feet against pavement, hurrying. Jane breathes relief for him.

Ned isn't around. She ditched Ned this evening, for Ned became a downer. She did some work on the piece after the hike, took a shower, and they met at the bar around eight. It was Friday night and she wanted to meet people. She mentioned Ned's band, how great it would be to see them play, maybe she could plug them in the magazine. Ned responded it wouldn't be possible—they had recently gotten back from a tour, he said, and none of them could stand to look at each other for weeks after a tour. She later learned by "tour" Ned meant a weekend stint in Cape Breton.

But publicity, enticed Jane.

"We're not really into that sort of thing," replied Ned.

She waited for more but he just looked around the bar, scratching, sweat-moons in the armpits of his shirt.

Jane wanted a Guinness, stood up to get it, but Ned motioned for her to sit, waving a waitress over simultaneously. Jane felt thwarted, her butt was sore from sitting. They were alone at their table, a cramped table for two, crowd roiling on either side of them. Where were all Ned's friends?

"My legs are killing me," he groused.

"What?" said Jane. "From the walk?"

"Yeah."

She picked up one of his cigarettes and pointed at him with it. "You should be doing that sort of thing every day, Ned."

He smiled and looked away from her again. Jane felt bored. "Where does all that Guinness enter into your fitness routine?" he asked after a moment.

Jane stretched. "The whole point of the routine is to be able to drink the Guinness. That's the whole point of everything, at the end of the day. This is how we orchestrate our lives."

"You talk about 'everything' a lot," Ned said.

"Breadth of vision," replied Jane, thinking of Marconi. "As alcoholics, we have a responsibility to see the big picture. We have to be unflinching. We can't afford to lie to ourselves about what it is we're engaged in exactly."

Ned looked worried. His eyebrows, already joined, bunched up in the middle.

"I mean we're engaged in drinking, yes, on the surface." She leaned forward. "Over-drinking. Self-medication. But we have to be precise about why that is, don't you think? If we're going to withdraw from the world, we'd better have damn good reasons why—if, *if* you accept that's what it is we're doing. We'd better be able to rhyme off those reasons if called upon to do so. If people accuse us of being afraid, we can explain that fear is a perfectly reasonable response to the world in which we live. The trick is, we can't be afraid of being afraid. We can't cower behind locked doors with our gin bottles and our arms across our eyes, if you know what I mean."

Jane waited for Ned to say something and stop looking worried. She added, "I think about this stuff a lot," almost by way of apology. "I'm thinking of writing a book or doing a blog or something."

"Who would wanna read a book like that?" Ned asked in a naked sort of way.

"You know, Ned," said Jane, stretching again. "I think I'll get going."

He nodded, pinched his eyebrows together some more, and stood up to walk her to the hotel. Jane waved him back down. Had to use both hands, stand there pushing air for five minutes at least.

"I THOUGHT," HE says, "you'd like to see an iceberg."

She sits up, adrift in the king-size bed, says nothing, then forces a yawn into the receiver just to let him know it's kind of early to be calling. "I've already seen the icebergs," she says in a voice like she's packing, or blowing languidly on her nails. "I've pretty much got everything I need."

"No but my brother can take us," says Ned. "He's got a boat."

"Can take us where?" asks Jane, stiffening for some reason.

"Out to see the icebergs."

"To? He can take us to them?"

"To," says Ned. "Right *to* 'em."

"When?"

"Day after tomorrow."

"Oh, Ned, I leave tomorrow morning."

"I know," says Ned. "But that's the only day he can do it."

"Why?" says Jane.

"Why?" Ned repeats, stymied. "I don't know, you'll have to ask him."

"I can pay him," says Jane.

"No, no, no, no," goes Ned, all east coast hospitality again.

"No, but, like, to go today or tomorrow, if it's a matter of money or something, I'll just pay him."

"It's not that," says Ned. "He's just busy doing something. It has to be day after tomorrow."

"Well, shit," says Jane.

"Can't you get your ticket changed?"

Jane hasn't thought of that. It would have to be on her own dime. Then there's the extra night at the Delta.

"I guess I could," she says. "It might be pricey. I may have to take you up on that offer to sleep on your couch."

"Good-good," says Ned.

She packs her bags, tucks away her laptop and bids a fond farewell to the hotel room, which she leaves a bedlam of newspapers and empty Evian bottles. She's been careful to dispose of her liquor empties when out and about, however, dropping them—wrapped up in plastic bags or newspapers—into the first garbage can she comes across on her way to get coffee. So the worst the chambermaids can say of Jane is that she hasn't caught the recycling bug.

They drink three bottles of wine over dinner before Ned starts rooting around under the sink for his harder stuff. This is the nicest time they've had together so far— it's because they're not in public, they can let their hair down and drink as much and as fast as they are inclined. They sit at the kitchen table all night, pouring and talking. They are kitchen-table drunks by nature, Jane realizes — the two of them, for all their combined bar-hopping. This is what they do. This here, as Ned would say.

The drunker Jane gets, the more she remembers the dream — floating out amongst the icebergs in the cool, clear water. She's fearless of a hangover, the dream fortifies and reassures her, tells her everything will be cool, clear sailing from here on out. Ice clinks into her glass and she touches it, imagines reaching out, wobbling to keep balance in Ned's brother's boat — she's been picturing a dory, which is probably ridiculous — hand stretching toward the monolith of ice. She fishes the ice cube from her drink, cups it in her palm, holds it to her face, then eyes. Against her eyes, it starts to melt in earnest.

Jean's problem? Jean Rhys? She expected such comfort from people, men.

Jane bursts out laughing, pops the lessened ice cube in her mouth.

"What's that?" asks Ned as if she's said something, smiling at her.

Jane shakes her head. She's embarrassed, ashamed, though she's always instructing herself never to feel this, about anything.

"The symbolism," she laughs. "I just realized how obvious it is."

Ned smiles and pats her hand like grandpa. It's that stage of drunkenness where you either accept that you understand nothing, or assume that you understand everything. He heads to the cupboard for a bag of Cheetos. Jane crunches more ice, something draining out of her. She feels panic at its going away. She's read that Freud treated people with recurring dreams—good and bad. He made them talk and talk about the dream until finally the patient understood precisely what was going on in his or her own head. The moment they did, the dream would depart. Freud drew back the curtain. He was like Toto, the yappy little rat who took the magic out of Oz.

Ned turns, sees her face. "No!" he says, putting the Cheetos aside. He goes to her, stands her up. "No!" he says again, her head between his big musician's hands.

THEY'LL SET OFF after lunch. Meanwhile, he's said she will need clothes even warmer than what she wished she had put on for Signal Hill. The wind off the water and all that. Fortunately, they won't have to putt-putt too far out into the open ocean, as the twins are situated just at the lip of the narrows. Still, Ned said, it will be "cold enough." And no doubt the wind will be good.

She rises early, Ned still asleep in his room. She insisted on the couch after the head-in-hands thing. Her mood is bereft. The day is blinding. She needs fresh air, cleansing wind. Coffee. Not to be in Ned's house, ashtrays on every surface.

More than anything, she wants to feel good, anticipatory. *Today's the day we go and see the icebergs.*

The only place she knows to go for clothes is downtown, but the only stores she can find are meant for suckers

from away, like her. One of the stores has a poster of the
movie in its window, claims to have been the "out-fitter."
Nobody dresses like that, she remembers, and she thinks
about Ned in his brown Doc Martens, the locals in their
Gore-Tex. She's even passed a few goths on Duckworth
Street. Still, some of the sweaters are gorgeous. One-
hundred percent virgin wool, and upwards of two hundred
dollars. She wants one. She treats herself. This is to go and
see the icebergs in.

The young cashier rings it up. Jane can see holes in her
face from which jewellery has been removed.

"You're the lady from the magazine," the hole-faced
girl accuses, folding the massive sweater into an ungainly
woolen lump.

Jane stares at her. "Yes."

"Dad was saying you're looking to go out on the boat."

"Dad?" says Jane, jaw to floor. "Ned?"

The kid laughs. "Oh, God help us, no. Ned's my uncle."

"Oh!" says Jane, and they laugh together at the mis-
understanding, though Jane doesn't know why.

"We hoped you would come out to supper," remarks
the girl. She's sixteen at the most, with an easy, middle-
aged way to her, leaning on the counter like a seen-it-all
waitress with varicose veins—for whom talking to strangers has long ago lost its sense of adventure.

"I'd be happy to come to supper," says Jane. Native hospitality at last, and just in time to save the article.

The kid frowns a stagey sort of frown, poking out her
lower lip. "Well, Ned said you couldn't. He said you were
busy."

Jane blinks. "I'm the farthest thing from busy."

"Oh," says the kid, sounding almost disappointed. "We were all set to give you shit. Say you want a last-minute boat ride and won't even come to supper."

"But I want to come to supper," Jane insists.

"When? I'll call mum."

"Well, how about after the boat ride? I know your dad is busy these next couple of days, so whenever is good for him."

The kid straightens her back, turns from middle-aged waitress into impudent youngster with a twist of her mouth. "Dad's not busy," she scoffs. "It's off-season."

"Oh." Jane pauses, the hangover-brain grinding to life. "What business is your father in?"

The kid gapes. Leans forward a little with her body. Enunciates word for word. "He gives people rides. In his boat."

SHE DRIFTS INTO the street, wanting sunglasses to fend off the bright of the sidewalk. Meanders to the end of the block and turns down toward Water Street as per the girl—Raylene's—instructions. The sign is big, hand-painted. An obtrusive sandwich-sign, meant to impede pedestrian traffic. "Dave's Charters." Inside is Dave, sitting behind his counter, cap pushed back on his head, and idly surfing the internet. Raylene's father. Brother of Ned. As tall as Ned is burly, but with the same bunching eyebrows.

He jumps up at the sound of the door—someone has stationed a too-large set of wind-chimes above it. They jangle around like the sound of madness. "Hi," Jane shouts above the chimes.

"Ah," says Dave. "It's she-who-wouldn't-come-to-supper." He stands, semi smiles. All Ned's family behave as if they've known her forever, and furthermore do not approve.

"I understand you're very busy," apologizes Jane.

Dave squints, frowning the same puckered, stagey frown with which his daughter favoured her moments ago. "My dear," says Dave. "I'm busy going broke."

Dave has several photographs for sale. Shots of the tower, the batteries that dot the hill—guns toward the water—the icebergs, reprints of the old Marconi photos. Quality reproductions in deliberately rough, wooden frames. Overpriced. Jane pretends to study them, giving the hangover-mind time to catch up. What Ned told her versus what he told them. And why. And why? Eventually buying two of the things by way of apology, once the gears have clicked more firmly into place. To make up for cancellation of the boat ride, but also the fact that she—just remembered!—can't make dinner this evening after all. She's got a flight to catch. Also she must make up for the fact that she was, apparently, staying directly across the street from Dave and family the whole time she was here. Dave with the long "a" sound in his name, across the street from her hotel.

Because, no. No indeedy, Ned. I will not do this thing with you.

Yet kept insisting, apparently, she'd have no time for a visit. No time for anyone but Ned. Then all of a sudden demanding a ride in the boat! This, she's gathered from

Dave's gruffness, is not how things are done. She selects a third print to take home, apologizing numbly all the while. It's cutting little salt with Dave. He'll be on the phone the moment she jangles her way out the door. Alerting local media. *West Coasters Big for Britches, As Suspected All Along.*

The prints of Marconi are the same images she saw at the tower for the most part. Different vantages of the same scenario; the photographer must have circled him, hoisting his heavy tripod around, ducking his head beneath a black shroud. The serene fanatic seated in his desolate, wind-blasted room at the top of the hill, wire-mess of his obsession on the table in front of him. A scribble of potential—connection unconnected. Oh, this? This is nothing.

HELLGOING

HELLGOING

Once she got back Theresa told her friends about how her father said she was overweight not even an hour into the visit. Just—boom, *you're fat*, he lays this on her. "Not, you know," said Theresa, "you look well, or you look healthy or, you know, maybe: however you might look, it's good to see you." Her friends held their faces and smiled in pain, the same way her brother had when he was sitting across the kitchen table from her with their father hunched and slurping tea between them.

Her brother had been her enemy once. Even though it was just the two of them, and only a year's difference in their age, they had never been the kind of siblings who were each other's greatest ally and defender. They weren't really each other's greatest enemy either—just petty rivals, but the rivalry was immediate and ongoing. The longer Theresa had been away as an adult, however, the nicer and better-adjusted Ricky seemed to get.

She had expected the worst when he decided to move

in with their father after their mother's death and Ricky's divorce. She had expected the two men, who were so alike already, to simply merge into one horrific masculine amalgam. And end up one of those bachelor pairs of fathers and sons that she knew so well from back home, finishing each other's sentences, eating the same thing every day — cereal, cheddar, toast, bologna with ketchup — pissing in the kitchen sink because the bathroom was too far away, wiping their hands on the arms of their chairs after finishing up a meal of cereal and cheese. Served on a TV tray. A TV tray never folded and put away, never scrubbed free of solidified ketchup puddles, never not stationed in front of the chair.

But Ricky got better instead of worse — he'd refused to merge into the two-headed, tea-slurping father-thing that haunted Theresa. Maybe it had haunted Ricky too, that bogeyman — perhaps he'd steeled himself against it. He had taken to wearing ironed, button-front shirts, for example, clean ones, even around the house, instead of T-shirts and sweats. He didn't wear a ball cap anymore, which was astounding because Theresa had never seen him out of one since seventh grade — he'd spent adolescent eternities in front of the hallway mirror attempting to get the curve of the brim just right.

Theresa arrived in their childhood home to find things neat, dust-free and zero TV trays in sight. Their father was expected to come to the table when his tea was ready — he didn't get it brought to him, like their mother would have done. "I'm not here to wait on ya, buddy," Ricky would call into the living room. "Get your arse to the table." He somehow had made it a new ritual from what it was when their mother was alive—something tougher, less domestic. Just a couple of dudes drinking tea. As if coming to the table was now a minor challenge thrown down from son to father, like their dad would be sort of a pussy if he didn't rise to the occasion. She wanted to applaud at that first sight of the old man heaving himself to his feet without so much as an irritated grunt. She wanted to take her brother aside and congratulate him on it.

She told a potted version of all this to her girlfriends as they sat around drinking vodka gimlets—they were on a gimlet kick—in Dana's living room. To set them up for the climax of the story, the big outrage: *Put on a few pounds, didn't ya?* She used the pissing in the sink line to make them smile, but also to ensure they had a solid sense of where Theresa and her father stood. Ruth's father, by way of contrast, was a provincial supreme court justice, long divorced, and he and Ruth went on cruises together to a different part of the world every year, where they had pictures taken of themselves holding hands.

Theresa had packed off her girls to their dad's house and flown home for the Thanksgiving long weekend. It was a long way to come for three days, but Ricky called her and asked her.

"Jeez, Ricky," she'd said on the phone, "I'd love to, but we're into mid-terms now. I'd planned on spending the whole time marking."

"With Mom gone," Ricky interrupted—it didn't feel like an interruption so much as an ambush, a bludgeoning. He silenced her by breaking the rules of their brother–sister interactions as she'd understood them up to this point. Theresa had been busy making her breezy, half-assed excuse and out of nowhere Ricky hits her with the grotesque reality of *with Mom gone.*

"With Mom gone," said Ricky, "I feel like we all have to make an extra effort here."

For years, she and Ricky were not in touch. They weren't estranged, it just never occurred to them to call each other. They sent Christmas cards, some Christmases. It took Ricky forever to get the hang of email, but once he was on email, they emailed. Ricky "wasn't much for typing," though. So they didn't email very often. Point being, Theresa knew what Ricky was saying in evoking their lack of mother—he was acknowledging that they had for years depended on their mother to give a shit on everybody else's behalf. Their mother giving a shit was the only thing that kept the family together. It was their mother who, at Christmas, made sure everyone had a present for everyone else. It was their mother who always passed the phone to Ricky when Theresa called on Christmas Eve. Their mother gave Theresa Ricky's news throughout the year (the divorce, the knee operation) and gave Ricky Theresa's (the divorce, tenure).

"The women of our mothers' generation," Theresa said to her friends. "That's what they do, right? That's their job—to give a shit so the rest of us don't have to bother—"

Jenn was sprawled on the loveseat shaking her head tightly as she spat an olive pit into her palm. "I get so mad, I get so mad," she interrupted. "My mom hauling out the address book every year and writing Christmas cards to everyone she's ever met in her life. I mean it takes her *days*. Then she carries them all over to Dad's chair for him to sign. It just—it infuriates me! Like he's had to put any effort into it whatsoever. Gavin—he doesn't get why it pisses me off so much when I'm sending a present to his mom or someone. He always goes, Hey, can we go in on that together? And I'm like, No, we fucking can't! I went *shopping* for your *mother*. I put actual *thought* into it. It took me an *afternoon* of my own *free time*! And I bought her a *card* and I *wrapped* the present and I'm going to drop it off at the *post office*. Do you know why *you* didn't do any of that? Because it's a pain in the ass! It's *effort*! But now you wanna get in on it? No! Go and get your mother a present *yourself* if you want to send her a present."

Everybody laughed. Jenn was playing up her anger for effect, because who among them hadn't tried to get in on someone else's present, piggybacking on another, better person's kindness? Her friends were being angry in solidarity with Theresa, dredging up their own slights and outrages and laying them neatly down like place settings—napkins, knives and forks.

"So what happens when women stop giving a shit?" asked Ruth then, trying to turn things into a seminar all of a sudden. You could always hear the 'y' when Ruth said "women"—*womyn*. Just like she wrote it. They all loved Ruth, but she never "punched the clock," as Dana liked to say. Her students all adored her, because she was like them—what her friends referred to, in private, as a "true believer."

Theresa spoke next in order to shut Ruth down—to

avoid the classroom discussion her question was meant to provoke and get back to her story. "The real question is," she said, "what happens when they all die off, our mothers?"

It was not the nicest way to get things back on track. Everyone else's mother but Theresa's was still alive, so every brow but her own was pinched in existential dread. But at least the attention was back on Theresa. This was her particular gift, she knew, after years of running seminars and sitting on panels. She knew how to manipulate the attention of others—to get it where she needed it to be. She knew how to be ruthless when she had to and she knew this was a trait she had inherited.

"What happens, I guess," said Theresa, "sometimes at least, is that people, sons, step up, the way Ricky has."

Ricky saw what a motherless future might hold and, by God, he took the helm. Yes, he moved in with a parent, but at least he didn't wear a ball cap anymore. (He must have looked in the mirror one day and thought: This is ridiculous. The hair is gone and everyone knows it.) And he hired a housekeeper to come in once a week—a masterstroke. And the housekeeper, she laundered the flowered armchair covers Theresa's mother had sewn years ago precisely in response to her husband's habit of wiping his food-smeared hands on the arms of the chair. It all meant that clean, orderly adulthood continued apace on Ricky's watch, with or without a mother on hand. Theresa had been fully braced for everything in her childhood home, including the dregs of her family (because what was her mother if not the best of their family, the cream, and what were Ricky, her father and Theresa herself if not the grounds at the bottom of the cup), to have gone completely to hell. But things had not gone to hell.

"Ahem," said Ricky, as they walked together down the dirt road to check the mailbox. "You don't have to sound, you know, quite so astounded."

She didn't tell this part to her friends—what she did to Ricky after what her father did to her. They walked down the road together, Theresa still vibrating. She'd been mugged, once, in Miami while taking a smoke break outside the hotel where her conference was being held, and she'd vibrated like this, exactly like this, after having her bag wrenched out of her hands by a scabbed meth-head who'd called her *cunt box*. "Cunt box?" Theresa had repeated in disbelief, trying to catch the meth-head's eye as they struggled—and that's when she lost her bag, because she'd been more focused on trying to prompt the scabbed man to elaborate than on maintaining her grip.

She was forty-four. *I am forty-four!* she'd sputtered at her father. She had had babies. *I have had babies! Put on some pounds? I've put on some pounds?*

Theresa had jumped out of her chair so fast it fell over. Goosed by insult—the shock of the insult, the unexpectedness of the attack. Her father sat there looking affrontedly at the overturned chair as Ricky ran a hand over his bristled head, maybe wishing for his ball cap, wishing for a brim with which to fiddle. The truth is, Theresa wanted to run across the yard into the wall of pines at the edge of her father's property, there to hide and cry.

She was the Assistant Chair of her department. She had

a paper coming out in *Hypatia*. She was flying to Innsbruck, Austria, in the spring to deliver that very paper. There would be another conference in Santa Cruz a few months later where she was the keynote motherfucking speaker. She was being flown down there. *I am being flown down*, she'd hacked, asphyxiating on the rest of the sentence.

"However," Theresa narrated to her friends, "who gives a shit about any of that, right? The important thing I need to know is I'm a fat piece of crap."

"Don't say that," pleaded Ruth. "Don't say 'I'm fat,' because then it's like you're agreeing with him, you're affirming it on some level."

Dana leaned forward. "Did you have an eating disorder when you were a kid?"

"*Of course* I had an eating disorder," yelled Theresa. "Who didn't have an eating disorder?"

"They push our buttons," said Jenn. "The buttons are installed at puberty and they can push them whenever they want."

"I didn't think I had the buttons anymore," said Theresa.

"We always have the buttons," said Dana.

"*They fuck you up, your mom and dad*," quoted Jenn.

It was an obvious quote, there was no other quote in the world more appropriate to quote at that moment, but Ruth jerked around, frowning. Disappointed at Jenn, because feminists weren't supposed to quote the likes of Philip Larkin. Theresa and Dana fired a secret *true-believer* grin at each other. Theresa was finally feeling like herself again.

She didn't tell her friends about anything else—the climax of the story had been told: *Put on a few pounds, didn't ya?* Ba dum *bump.* Punchline! She didn't tell them how she tried to offload her feelings onto Ricky as they walked the dirt road. He was only trying to make her feel better with the walk. But she kept jawing on about how great the house looked, how well their father seemed ("Same old Dad!"), how monumental it was that Ricky made him get up from in front of the TV and come to the table. And hiring a housekeeper—how had he known where to look? Then it just seemed natural that she move on to Ricky himself— he was looking great! He'd stopped smoking, she noticed. He seemed so fit, so together. She was getting personal now. Was he running? Going to the gym? He was dressing better, wasn't he—had that been, like, a conscious deci- sion at some point? When had he ditched the ball cap—she had to be honest, that was a good call. Just shave the head, rock the bald-guy thing. Everyone was doing it these days. He was looking, she told him—forty-four-year-old divor- cee sister to forty-three-year-old divorcee brother—very grown up.

Which was when he told her she did not have to sound quite so astounded by it all.

She used to do this to her mother, she remembered abruptly. Because she didn't have the nerve to retaliate against her father, she would torment her mother instead. Ricky had never done that, she was sure. He protected their mother. He absorbed things like a sponge, whereas Theresa had always needed someone to pay.

"Sorry," said Theresa.

"I was married for many years," said Ricky.

"Sure, I know," said Theresa.

"So I know how to run a home, is what I'm saying."

She realized she knew nothing about her brother's married life. The woman's name was June, they had eloped to Vegas (according to Theresa's mother, who'd told her over the phone) and so there wasn't even a wedding to attend, no in-laws to meet. June was a cashier at Ricky's pharmacy. Theresa had to admit she hadn't taken a huge interest in June. The last she heard about their activities as a couple, just before she heard about the divorce, was that they'd bought a speedboat.

"June," said Ricky, "struggled with depression."

He said it like an ad, a PSA. Like he had read many pamphlets, posters on a doctor's wall.

"Oh," said Theresa.

"Sometimes she would go to bed for weeks."

"Whoa," said Theresa. "Jeez."

"So that was shitty," he sighed.

And now you live with Dad? Theresa wanted to say. Now you reward yourself by moving in with Dad?

"It just made me see how easy it is for people to give up," said Ricky. "You have to be vigilant."

"Yeah," said Theresa. "Well —" She had nothing insightful to say to her brother. She'd spent her life being vigilant about other things. You can only be vigilant, she thought, about a few things at a time. Otherwise it's not vigilance anymore. It starts to be more like panic.

"Well, I just think it's great, Ricky. I mean—good for you. Really."

Ricky sighed again. They had arrived at the mailbox. As they were approaching it, Theresa could see the flag wasn't up. But they walked the rest of the distance anyway and Ricky rested his hand on the box like it was the head of a faithful dog.

"You wanna check?" he said.

This was sudden childhood. The walk to the mailbox. The peek inside for mail-treasure. Because sometimes, Theresa remembered, the postman just forgot to put the flag up. Or it fell down on its own, but the mail remained within. That was the earliest lesson, when it came to vigilance, the giddiest lesson. You flew to the end of the road no matter what the flag was doing, you didn't hesitate, you stood up on your toes and had a look either way. You could never trust the flag.

DOGS IN CLOTHES

DOGS IN CLOTHES

You'll be glad to get out of here, they all told Marco moments after shaking his hand, inviting him to sit down at the microphone. How long are you in town for? And Marco would tell the host, or producer, or whoever it happened to be, the same thing he'd been saying all morning: in and out, quick trip, reception last night, lecture tonight, flight to London first thing tomorrow.

But in the myopic way of local media, the host or producer always wanted the small talk to be about the city. What was happening in the city. The police fences going up and latest restrictions announced. Something on the car radio this morning about no flying kites downtown. Kites would be banned the week of the convention, the radio announced, deadpan. Sam had leaned forward to hear better but Marco was not a morning person. His eyes were closed and his cheek vibrated against the passenger's side window.

I live in Washington, he yawned when Sam exclaimed

about the kites. There's police everywhere. You get used
to it.

But people are allowed to fly kites in America, said Sam.

Not since 9/11, said Marco.

He was renowned for what they called his "dry wit." It
surprised people, when they met him, because his writing
wasn't dry. His writing was wet. It flowed with emotion
and swelled with profundity and was boundless in its eru-
dition according to the press kit on the seat between them.
Sam didn't laugh at Marco's remark, however, because his
dryness in conversation entailed that he didn't drop any of
the usual hints of *this is a joke; laugh with me, won't you?* —
didn't attempt to catch her eye, or smirk. Or, as Sam might
have done, sound a giddy little snort.

Yesterday she learned to smile in a neutral sort of way
at everything Marco said on the off-chance he was making
a crack of some kind and she hadn't caught it. It was safe.
She hit upon the strategy not long after picking him up at
the airport and used it to great effect at the reception that
evening—she used it with everybody, not just Marco. It
was a handy trick. She blank-smiled not only the lumin-
aries who came out to greet Marco—flashy silver-hairs in
colourful scarves (the men) whose names she understood
she was supposed to recognize the moment they were
enunciated at her—but even the blowsy female editor
who intimidated her and the philanthropist CEO who was
always so courtly and drunk.

There was something about smiling in a neutral way at
people that sort of impressed them, she discovered. *I give
you nothing*, it told them, which they liked. It made them

notice her, whereas in the past, whenever she'd attempted some bland, quippy remark, they all but tried to rest their drinks on her head.

For Samantha was short.

She settled in behind the glass with the producer and technicians and checked her phone and found a text from her brother sitting there.

At hospital. Pre-op stuff.

She poked back: *Ok! xoxo*

The host had asked Marco to talk about whatever for a moment or two; what he had for breakfast, for example, so that the technician could get his levels. I don't eat breakfast, Marco was saying. Mornings make me sick.

Just anything, urged the host.

Sam had heard this before from the radio people. Radio people didn't get it because they were so used to talking— filling the airwaves on command. But it was dumb to ask the guest to talk about whatever. Guests needed specifics. The concept "whatever" ballooned in their minds, which accordingly went blank.

Then she saw her brother had sent the text three hours ago and realized she'd had her phone muted since the night before and thanked God Marco wasn't a morning person and hadn't been calling at 6 a.m. wanting a power smoothie or something.

She texted her brother again: *So updates?*

Marco had his headset on and the levels were good and now he was saying: We desire. It's what humans do. We want to open doors, tear at packages, hammer piggy banks, rip bodices. It's an essential force and an essentially destructive force. We have to reconcile ourselves.

The light was low in the studio; it was an artificial environment, meant to fake a feeling of end-of-day serenity, as if outside birds were peeping wearily and lawns were perspiring dew.

She watched Marco on the other side of the glass, saying versions of other things he had already said that morning. Eventually his words coagulated into a mellifluous white noise and for something to do she texted Marie.

Marco in a gorilla cage.

It was the idea of sticking him in an artificial environment. Marco peeling bamboo as the popcorn-eating masses gawked. Explaining to them in gorilla sign-language: *We desire.*

Although a voiceless Marco clearly would be not the same sort of Marco at all.

Mar-Koko, she texted next. Sam often texted stream-of-consciousness to Marie.

I'd take him in any kind of cage, replied Marie, who was always insisting upon her thing for older men. Sam had come to find this boring about her.

This is what it means to be fallen creatures, Marco was saying. In the biblical sense.

It was the fourth time she'd heard him make this statement and she still didn't understand what it meant. The phrase wheeled around in her head, clanging, like a pot-lid dropped and spinning across a kitchen floor.

You want to know him biblically, she texted Marie.

Then her brother wrote: *He went into OR hour ago.*

She texted: *Agh! Tx! xoxo*

Ew, wrote back Marie. *Evangel-lovin'. Give it up for JC.*

It was a short interview because it was live and live segments always had to be short, Sam had observed, to keep people from tiring out and saying something stupid on the air. Marco was coming to the end and then they would go for lunch. Sam texted Marie: *The Bible is very dirty. Compendium of sin. A very dirty and vicious place.*

Marco had removed his headset and was shaking hands with the host.

Sign me up, said Marie.

THE BLOWSY EDITOR was meeting them at something called an Izakaya restaurant, which had just opened up around the corner from the office. She and Marco were late, however, because the route Sam planned on taking had been blocked off by a police fence.

But this is right in the middle of downtown, complained Marco, scrutinizing the chain-link and concrete beyond. It doesn't make any sense.

I guess there's going to be, like, said Sam, who didn't really know what she was talking about, a security zone or something.

But people will still need to get from point A to point B during the convention, said Marco. Are they planning to evacuate downtown?

Finally he was showing an interest in what was going on in the city and the only person there to explain it was Sam, who had only started paying attention that morning when she heard about the kites.

She gave a neutral smile. Ideally, she said, that's probably what they'd like to do. Evaporate.

As she said it, she realized she'd meant to say "evacuate." But Marco didn't notice.

People get in the way, he agreed.

THEY WERE FIFTEEN minutes late and when they arrived the entire restaurant staff yelled something at them in Japanese, startling Sam. She looked around in a panic, but everybody, after yelling, just went back to cooking and chopping and waitressing as if nothing had happened. The editor was seated at the far end of the restaurant, gesturing with both hands, her gauzy sleeves billowing like sails.

Don't tell me, she said, brushing cheeks with Marco. Police fences.

Just everywhere, said Marco.

Well, don't worry, said the editor. The service here is like nothing you've ever seen. Sam? When is Marco's next appointment?

Sam already had her phone in her hand. *Still on the table, no news*, her brother had written.

Not until two, she said.

Lots of time, said the editor.

Sam leaned back and placed her phone beside her napkin as the editor leaned forward to ask Marco how his morning interviews had gone. The moment the phone touched the tabletop it lit up with another text.

It was nice to see you last night.

So she yanked it back up and read it again. She typed: *You suck, texting me,* and stuffed the phone in her purse.

It's okay, Sam, if you need to keep your phone out, the editor told her, glancing over. Which was a way of saying, Shouldn't you keep your phone out? Because to be in constant contact was Sam's job. She gave a neutral smile and placed the phone beside her chopsticks. Sam could feel her ears producing a heat that would soon make her entire face look boiled.

She wanted to text Marie about it. Marco and the editor were leaning toward each other in order to hear and be heard over all the restaurant noise. Both of them had their hands resting on the edge of the table. It was like they were preparing to play the mirror game.

Marco was saying: The idea that we are in the way. In the way of nature, like Sartre said. Perhaps that's what it is to exist.

And is it a bad thing, necessarily, said the editor.

But the problem is, we treat everything *else* that way.

So who's in the way?

The more important question is, who gets to decide?

When they hugged the night before at the reception. And the side of her head was warm against Alex's breastbone, her ear squashed against him as if to ask, You in there? Anybody home? And it was longer than it should have been, the hug, yes, full of heat. And Natalie was there who was his wife. And then they just got on with the evening, making the rounds and paying attention to other people and not to each other as they had long agreed to do.

Which is why it sucked of him to text her.

Excuse me, said Sam, and left for the bathroom.

Very dirty and vicious place, was the last thing she had written to Marie.

Ugh, she texted now.

What, wrote Marie.

Alex, wrote Sam.

Yikes, wrote Marie. *Is he there?*

Texted.

Ignore it. Delete message.

You know you are a good person, added Marie a moment later.

Her brother wrote, *About halfway through and all is well so far. One end of bypass connected. They are now sizing the new tissue valve.*

Sam could picture him hunched on some bench in some waiting room, taking forever to peck out the message with his slow, enormous man-thumbs. There was ten years between them. He hadn't exited the womb with a cellphone in hand the way she had. Texting was like breathing for Sam, or blinking her eyes, whereas for her brother it was exactly like poking away at infinitesimal buttons on a tiny little machine. It was like trying to thread a series of needles just to tell a person something.

The staff yelled at them again as they left the restaurant—even louder than when she and Marco had arrived. Sam had been thinking about her brother's giant thumbs and also Alex's hands and how she held one of her hands up against his one time and remarked how the size of women's hands compared to men's seemed like a deliberate, cosmic humiliation because when you really looked at them, when you compared and contrasted, women's hands were downright *puny*. So she had been looking at her hand around her phone as they left the restaurant thinking that it—her hand closed around an object—sort of resembled a big white grub or a giant scallop, and the staff hollering scared her even worse this time.

Why do they do that, Sam wanted to know.

Marco looked over at her—made a point of looking over at her, which was actually kind of touching. He hadn't really looked at her since they met the day before, even when he was telling her something.

Then she realized the editor had looked over at her too. It had to do with the way her question sounded—higher pitched than it probably should have been, drawing attention to itself.

They're just saying goodbye to us, sweetie, said Marco in the tender voice he used for interviews.

Sam realized she didn't know if she had eaten anything.

OUTSIDE ON THE sidewalk they were swarmed by young women in white shorts and yoga tops who were trying to give them hot sauce.

Want some hot sauce? They said. Free hot sauce!

Marco took one and handed it to Sam, who put it in her purse.

Hot sauce? Another of the girls said to Sam.

I just took some, Sam told her.

Have some more, insisted the girl. She was overtanned and grinning away, making a point of meeting Sam's eye as if they were flirting with each other. She'd been told to do this, Sam realized, had probably been staring into the eyes and grinning into the faces of countless strangers all day long. The girl was on auto-pilot.

So Sam accepted another bottle as Marco and the editor brushed cheeks goodbye. As the editor pulled away, a girl tried to give her hot sauce.

No, no, said the editor, moving down the sidewalk. Sam admired the easy way she held up her hand; easy, yet with authority — *That is the way you use a hand*, thought Sam — stopping the girl mid-proffer.

But Marco accepted the hot sauce on the editor's behalf and handed this one to Sam as well.

Moments after they'd disentangled themselves from the girls in white, Sam looked back to see a young policeman approaching the group. The girls fluttered whitely to intercept him like seagulls expecting to be fed.

Put the sauce away, girls, she heard the young cop say before she and Marco rounded the corner.

No kites and no sauce, Sam remarked as they approached the car.

Pardon? said Marco.

She shouldn't have said it out loud. It was the kind of thing she would have texted to Marie.

That cop, said Sam. He made the girls put away their sauce.

Well, thank God for that, said Marco.

THERE WAS JUST one more interview and then Marco was allowed to go back to the hotel for a nap or whatever he wanted to do before meeting up with everyone at the restaurant.

I hate when they make you have dinner before giving a talk, he told Sam when they were back in the car.

Sam herself was looking forward to the dinner because the restaurant was new and the fish was supposed to be insanely fresh and even the drinks would be paid for. That showed how impressive Marco was.

Best seafood in town, she told him.

Marco blinked his great, sad eyes. His eyes were so large, he seemed to blink in slow motion.

Those eyes, Marie had texted the day before.

I think he's gay, though, Sam told her. *He doesn't give off any heat.*

But you can't stuff yourself with seafood and then talk about the human soul, said Marco.

No? said Sam.

And the other thing, said Marco, is I won't be able to drink. Sorry to whine—I know I'm whining—but it's good to be a bit of a brat between interviews; to misbehave before I have to be all gracious and wise. I just like a glass of wine with meals.

You can't have a glass of wine before the talk?

I don't like to, no. Marco was gazing up at the building before them. Weren't we just here this morning?

That was live, Sam told him. This is taped. It'll be more in-depth, too, like a couple of hours give or take.

The police are out front now, observed Marco, noticing

cruisers all along the street. They're going to fence off the broadcasters. Smart move.

Sam gave a neutral smile.

HER PHONE HAD been vibrating intermittently in her purse like some tiny panicked creature and the technician frowned at her for taking it out because the three bottles of hot sauce made such a racket when she did. There's no microphone in here, Sam wanted to bark at him. Radioland can't hear my sauce. So keep your frowns to yourself.

There was a text from Marie wanting to know, *Did you text him back?* And a text from Alex saying, *Where are you living these days?* Which was a way of asking if she still had a roommate. Because all Alex ever had to say to her was a form of the question: Where can we fuck? Or else: When can we fuck? Or the statement: I assume we will be fucking shortly. Which was usually correct. And as she was pondering these questions and statements a message popped up from her brother which read: *Procedure complete, now undergoing post-maintenance testing.*

The interviewer was a woman this time, a woman with one of the best voices on the radio, a voice like nougat. She did not look at all like she sounded, which shouldn't have bothered Sam, she knew, but which did. The interviewer, who sounded like a sexy professor on the radio, looked like somebody's mad aunt in real life. She wore pink Crocs and velour pants covered in cat hair. Sam never thought of being middle aged—she tried not to—because it made her weepy, which in turn made her feel guilty. She knew she,

herself, could easily give in to velour and Crocs, she knew
how happy she might one day be made by cats, she knew
how simple it would be to let go, to have wrinkles appear
on her face and say: *Oh well—to hell with it then.* She could
do it in a heartbeat; she could give up on youth like it was
nothing. It was the easy way out, like a gun was, kind of.
Terrifying in the same way.

So she didn't think about it.

Marie kept texting in an effort to be a good friend. She
was texting: *Remember you are blameless.* And a couple of
minutes after that: *You made no promises or vows to anybody.*
And then: *No one expects anything of you.*

Sitting in the booth with the technician, Sam just
wanted to close her eyes and visualize the sexy professor as
the interviewer spoke, but her phone kept jumping and the
interviewer kept asking Marco questions and Marco kept
saying things like: We live in torment at our own carnivor-
ous nature. We are divided beings. We are shaped to feed
upon our fellow creatures, just as they are shaped to feed
one another. We tie ourselves in knots to avoid the reality.
We keep our butchers in the backroom, where we don't
have to view their work. We treat the people who feed us
like pariahs. We don't want to know. We are ashamed. We
can't abide the sin. We dress our dogs in clothes, like us. To
convince ourselves we are confreres.

When you say "sin"—began the nougat-voiced interviewer.

Sin! Interrupted Marco. And you've hit on it exactly. It
is the first sin, the ultimate sin. Historically, in religious
terms, we've supposed that sin was sex, but sex is just the

smallest part of it. The real anguish resides in our break with the animals. We don't want to harm them; yet we're made to harm them. This is why they are innocent and we can never be. We can *never* be. This is what it is to be human — to be human is to be fallen.

I'm not sure I get it, confessed the interviewer.

Sam, however — shifting forward, hot sauce chattering away in her purse — Sam got it.

BACK ON THE sidewalk, three policemen stood together watching them walk past.

Hello, said one to Sam.

Good afternoon, said Marco as Sam stalked past all four of them.

HE ASKED TO use her phone in the car, and then had to ask how to use it, and Sam wondered if he was one of those people who held up cellphone usage as an example of how the world was going to hell and vowed to never succumb, unlike the brainless masses, to such foolishness. Like the courtly CEO where Sam worked who had never not had secretaries to make his phone calls anyway. She tried not to stare at Marco while he spoke to whomever he was speaking to, but she wasn't succeeding. She just gave in and stared at him. She was getting the feeling that everything Marco said — be it to interviewers or the editor or the party on the other end of the phone — was the same thing. Was part, that is, of one long, unspooling thought that never

ended, that had no paragraph breaks, that refused to natur-
ally conclude, as in polite conversation. And nobody asked
him to give it a rest, nobody ever said, Yeah, okay, Marco,
but we are talking about going to the beach now. Nobody
broke in to ask what he wanted on his pizza.

Or if they did, Marco did not let himself get sidetracked.

Marco was saying, Don't give him that. Lovey, don't
give him that. I know he wants it, but don't give him that.
It's bad for him. No, it's up to you. You are the one in charge
and it is bad for him. Don't argue with me, lovey, this is
your responsibility. No, no, no. Okay? No. No no no.

Now Marco was noticing how Sam was neglecting to
pretend not to listen to him. She was driving, but she kept
looking over at every other word.

I hope that was okay, said Marco when he was finished,
holding the phone out to Sam. It was on my calling card.

Can you just stick it in my purse, please?

Marco opened her purse.

Look at all your hot sauce! he exclaimed.

SHE DROPPED MARCO off after battling the traffic and
negotiating countless new detours, and now only had an
hour until she picked him up again. So Sam walked to the
back of the hotel, where there was a park with benches
for people to sit and watch the ferries chug back and forth
across the lake.

She brought Marco's book along because she was supposed to have read it weeks ago.

She found a free bench and texted Marie.

Someone is messing with me. Someone is rattling my cage.

Then Alex wrote, as if in response, *I thought I'd go to the Marco thing tonight.*

He was one of those men who didn't wear deodorant and somehow got away with it. Or maybe he wore some kind of natural deodorant that didn't really mask his sweat. The point was, Sam could always smell him. It was not a bad smell; it was just entirely him, his bodily self-announcement. It was his presence; fulminating beneath his skin and emerging from his pores. You knew when he was there, and when he had been there.

Whenever that smell hit Sam, her uterus would contract with sudden violence. Like it was hurling itself against her abdomen in mute, uterine frenzy.

At the next bench, a man was seducing a woman and Sam could hear the occasional low-voiced inanity. I am the kind of person, he was saying to the woman, who is very aware of his energy.

A policeman on an actual horse appeared out of nowhere and clopped his way past Sam, claustrophobically close, a liquid wall of chestnut haunch.

This world brings entities together so they can feel joy, the man on the bench was saying.

The cop on the horse slowed its clop as he approached the couple. He was wearing a helmet, which Sam thought made good sense. It struck her that probably everyone who rode horses should wear helmets. Because who knew what a horse might do?

A text from her brother read: *Unfortunately it looks like—* before Sam stopped reading it and put her phone away.

She picked up Marco's book and opened to the first page. The cop was murmuring something to the man—the seducer—and what the cop was saying was making the man surprised. The seducer started speaking in high-pitched exclamations. Sam held the book in front of her face. After a moment or two she saw from her peripheral vision that the man, still exclaiming and gesturing, was getting to his feet.

The cop made some small, indeterminate movement—Sam couldn't say if it was a gesture or if the cop had physically made contact of some kind. Either way, the seducer sank back onto the bench.

SHE ORDERED ONE glass of red wine and one glass of white and carried them across the room to Marco. Then she had to stand there awhile and wait for him to distinguish and differentiate Sam's expectant presence from all the other expectant presences that had clustered around him after his talk.

Eventually his eyes did a tour of the circle of faces. Sam! he greeted.

Red or white? she mouthed.

Very kind, said Marco, allowing his soupy brown eyes to pour appreciation into hers. He reached for the white.

Sam blank-smiled and brought the red to her own lips, holding his eye as she receded from the cluster. Marco, looking stymied, watched her go. He was paying extra attention now because of the way she had behaved in the car and in the restaurant. She hadn't said much. But she'd said enough to let him know her feelings toward him were taking on a purplish tinge of the unprofessional.

Sam, called Marco before she had completely receded from the circle. You don't have to disappear.

The members of Marco's conversational klatch were now gazing like cows back and forth between Marco and Sam with a total lack of interest. Waiting brainlessly for the exchange to be over.

I'm not going anywhere, Sam assured Marco.

She turned and walked directly into Alex's looming chest. Her wine sloshed and some of it splattered to the floor, but somehow didn't get anywhere on him, which was so typical. The smell — like fresh pelt — hit her hard. She craned her neck to peer up at him and her uterus shook itself awake like a dog.

Clumsy, said Alex, whose one-note mode of flirtation had always been personal insult. She understood then the whole affair had been about efficiency. This was how you sinned and took your punishment all at once.

He smiled down at Sam, allowing his smell to settle all around her.

What? Sam said.

What? said Alex back.

Here was yet another easy way out — like stepping off a cliff. Sam cleared her throat in order to be heard.

"When can we fuck?" she said.

Alex's eyes actually bulged and he hunched forward, abruptly telescoping his height in a way that appeared spastic and involuntary. *Whoa, whoa, whoa!* he whispered. If he had been carrying some kind of sack around with him, he might have thrown it over Sam's head.

She turned away from him to check her phone, ignoring the howls from her lower abdomen. There was another text from her brother, starting *Did you* — so she put it away and moved toward the bar.

MARCO IS AN animal, she had texted Marie during the talk. She'd been thinking he had eyes like moose: puzzled and stupid and bulgy. And his silky curls shining under the spotlight made her think of the poodle she had growing up; a poodle named Arfer. *Do tell!* Marie wrote back. Marie had her own interpretation of everything. Transmitting her thoughts to Marie was like cutting the string off a kite, allowing the wind to yank it around in any and every direction; relinquishing ownership.

And after they arrived at the dinner, the blowsy editor had approached her and said, Sam, I was trying to get in touch with you for the last hour to drop off something for Marco but I wasn't able to get through on your phone.

And Sam, who'd had her ringer turned off since the moment on the park bench with the police horse clopping past, stared at the editor's swelling jowls and told her, *My father was having his heart taken out.* And that was all she had to say, the editor didn't even let her finish. The editor's jowls drooped another couple centimetres — she was almost not middle-aged anymore, Sam abruptly realized; the editor was almost actually old — and she terrified Sam by lurching forward and holding Sam in her billowy arms a moment.

IT WAS VERY late in the evening when Marco sought her out. He had made it clear all day he wanted to be rested for the flight tomorrow morning. Don't let me linger too long, he instructed. And for the love of God, don't let me drink too much. Two, three glasses of wine. Don't let anyone put a glass of scotch in front of me, or I'm toast. I can't handle the jet lag the next day — at my age it's just crippling.

And Sam had ignored him for most of the night.

He found her at a table drinking with a couple of interns from another house. He had to lean past her chair and insert himself into the frothy, college-girl conversation, which was mostly gossip about older — but not too much older — colleagues where they worked. I think it's time to go, said Marco, sounding as if he was the one minding Sam instead of the other way around. She got up without a word — busily draining her drink as she stood — and followed him to the parking lot.

I shouldn't drive, I am completely shit-faced, explained Sam. But how about I call you a cab.

She grabbed her phone and saw there was a voicemail from her brother.

Actually, she told Marco, it's pretty easy to flag one down.

He gazed down the street. The hotel sign was blazing in the distance like a signal fire. It might be nice to walk, he said.

Oh, they'd kill me if I let you walk home by yourself.

Then, Sam, said Marco. Please don't let me walk home by myself.

They walked. Sam hobbled along for a moment, taking off her high heels, and went from being about even with

Marco's armpits to meeting him at mid-chest. Now she was at nipple height. Psychic text to Marie — *Hey Marie: nipple height.*

I want to say, Marco told her once Sam had worked her shoes off. I appreciate your care these past couple of days. I'm sorry, if I ever seemed distant at all.

Oh — distant, repeated Sam.

These junkets, continued Marco, they actually require a great deal of energy and concentration for me. I'm an introvert by nature. To be chauffeured around, speaking into microphones, getting up in front of crowds — it's wearing. I feel I have to conserve energy at every spare moment.

Uh-huh, said Sam.

Marco turned his liquid eyes toward the looming hotel sign, which didn't seem to be getting much bigger as they advanced. I'm saying if I was rude to you at any point. Or inconsiderate.

Sam waited. But Marco had stopped talking. He was just stopping there. He wasn't even going to finish the sentence.

Rude, repeated Sam.

Or inconsiderate. Of your feelings.

Sam sounded a giddy little snort.

Then I apologize, finished Marco at last, frowning like invisible fingers were actually pulling at his face; like it was painful, but he was helpless not to do it.

Sam noticed they were walking alongside a police fence. She fell against it briefly just to feel the metal and hear it jangle.

There is insult, Marco, said Sam. Insult is no problem.

I am insulted every day, by all sorts of people, because that is what it is to be short. That is what it is to be *human*, as you would say — ha ha. There is insult, and then of course there is full-scale attack.

Attack, repeated Marco.

I shouldn't say full-scale attack, no. I should say covert attack. Which is secret and dirty and vicious. And cowardly.

You think I, said Marco.

Sam's phone jumped in her purse, nuzzling away at her thigh through the leather.

It's all *couched*, Sam shrieked, piercing the night with the chipmunky, short-woman's voice she acquired whenever she became upset. She jerked a little when she shrieked, bouncing against the fence again and causing the three bottles of hot sauce, which she still hadn't taken out of her purse, to clack together like bones. Now Marco looked like he wanted to throw his hands over his ears. You sit there, said Sam, on the other side of the glass, *accusing* me while *pretending* I'm not there.

Not at all, said Marco, blinking his great eyes as rapidly as someone with such big eyes was capable.

And I started reading your book. I know I was supposed to read it before now, but I didn't. But I started just today, once I realized what you were doing. And I just can't believe it, Marco.

Something wet and warm fell into her cleavage. Sam knew it was her own saliva. She was drooling. She was drooling she was so angry.

Can't believe what? Marco pleaded, sounding distant and terror-struck.

He'd never imagined, perhaps, that Sam would ever settle down to thinking long enough to put it all together. He never dreamed she'd hold her ground, let alone come rampaging at him through the fences in full revolt.

TAKE THIS AND EAT IT

TAKE THIS AND EAT IT

Well, I keep seeing this girl now. The first time I saw her was terrible—her parents brought her in because she had stopped eating and she was in one of the rooms having a tube worked down her nose. I had paused on my way down the hall to visit Sylvia Embree dying of lung cancer because I could hear the doctors and nurses shuffling around, barking orders and crying out whenever one of her flailing limbs connected. And the girl, this little fourteen-year-old girl was shouting with great authority that Our Lord would bring down his wrath upon all their heads. She had such a deep and outraged voice for a child. I have to say I was impressed and stopped to take a peek.

The moment I stuck my nose in the door, young Dr. Pat looked up and told me, "Sister, you could help."

They'd never asked me to help before. I stepped over the threshold like a kitten.

"No, really, Sister," said Dr. Pat. "Please." He took his hand off the girl for a quick instant to wave me over. "Now

[71]

this is Sister Anita!" he yelled down at the girl, who was trying to yank the tube out of her face as Dr. Pat and a nurse kept hold of her arms.

She stopped struggling for a moment to take me in. Then nodded, all business. "Jesus is Lord," she said. Tried to butt the doctor with her forehead, then.

How about that, I couldn't stop my mind from saying.

Now she's a regular, like Sylvia Embree. I keep seeing her laid out there like an invalid, taking up one bed after another—in and out all the time. "For pity's sake, Catherine," I tell her, "this is getting ridiculous, a young girl like yourself. Have a bite to eat and get on with it."

For the most part, she ignores me. We spoke a little the first time she was admitted, and I think she's decided I'm a fraud or some such thing. Too low on the totem pole for the exalted likes of her. She told me she was fasting, just like the nuns do, and I asked did she want to become a nun. She just snorted at me like I'd asked did she want to become a clown in the circus, like she was insulted. Well, I was insulted too so I got up to go talk to Sylvia. Sylvia needs a machine to do her breathing for her and still she wouldn't quit the smokes if she had anything left to say about it. In a way, she and the girl are the same sort of specimen.

"Now, Sylvia," I tell her sometimes. "There's a girl down the hall who won't take a bite, she's starving herself. Killing herself deliberately."

"Well, the foolish thing."

"Yes, but will you look who's talking?"

But I only say that sort of thing when Sylvia's going on and on about her cigarettes.

"Why don't you just ask me to bring you a gun?" I'll tell her.

"One of these days I might," she's answered once or twice.

I should leave Sylvia alone about it. She's old and she's dying. But a fourteen-year-old girl—there's little excuse.

Still, it's none of my business. I don't want it to be. Once every few months I'll pass a room and there she'll be and I will call as I go by: "Not again!" But that's about all I have to say to her these days. I didn't particularly like her after that snort.

But then Dr. Pat takes me aside one day when Catherine's back on the ward and asks if I'll meet with him and the social worker, a woman named Hilary. I dart my eyes around for a moment, perhaps in the hope that someone else is going to step forward and say, No, no, no, I'll do it—what in God's name are you asking Anita for. But nobody does, so I say I suppose that I could.

This Hilary and I pass each other in the hall at different hours of the day. She carries her folders and I have my beads. She's young, but wears her glasses on a chain like someone's grammy. We nod on occasion.

"Catherine's condition is fairly bound up with her religion," Dr. Pat explains like I'm some kind of simpleton. Hilary and I sit side by side in front of his desk. Hilary swivels her chair around and looks at me the moment he says *religion*.

"So it would seem," I remark. Even though I don't need to, I untuck a piece of tissue from my sleeve and lightly blow my nose before the two of them. I suppose I'm a bit nervous.

"Have you spoken to her at all?" the social worker wants to know.

"I told her I found it ridiculous."

"Really?" says Hilary.

"Yes—and I do," I say.

"Well, would you mind talking to her a bit more?"

"I'd be happy to talk to her," I say. "But I thought that was your job."

"I thought it was your job too—" says Hilary.

We smile at each other. Two nice women.

"Well," interrupts Dr. Pat. "She's really quite obsessed with religion. We're hoping you could explain things to her. That, you know, God doesn't require she starve herself, basically."

"Well, I told her I thought it was nonsense. To be honest, she doesn't seem to have much respect for me. I expect she sees me as a bit of an anachronism." I look at Hilary and smile again.

"To be honest, Sister," she says, echoing me, "I find I just can't speak to Catherine on that level. I don't have the background. I don't have your expertise. She challenges me on all these points of doctrine, and what am I to say?"

"You're not Catholic," I say.

"I'm not religious at all," says Hilary. And the quick way she straightens her back shows me a woman who was baptized, took communion and knows the Act of Contrition by heart. She might as well be making the sign of the cross.

"In that case," I say—and I don't know why I am making this so hard for poor Hilary—"why not just tell her it's a bunch of hokum?" I twiddle my beads.

Hilary looks pained. "Sister," she appeals. "Catherine comes from a very devout family. Who am I to assail her faith?"

So off I go to talk to the little fanatic.

"So here we are," I say. "I'm supposed to sit here and talk to you about God."

"Whoop-de-shit," says the girl.

"Oh goodness the language," I say. "I'm certainly appalled."

She laughs a bit. Isn't this going well.

"So what do you want to starve yourself for?" I say. "Who told you to do that?"

"Nobody," says Catherine.

I'm surprised because I was sure she was going to tell me God did. "Well? What's the good of it then?"

"Well, that is what religious people do, isn't it?" says Catherine, reasonably enough. "Don't nuns fast?"

"You're not a nun."

"Jesus fasted."

"Well, you're not him either now, are you?"

"I'm devout," insists Catherine. "I'm just being devout."

"But you're hurting yourself, dear, just look at the size of you."

"Well, I don't care, I want to be the empty vessel. I want to be filled with God. I want him to fill me." She gets this look on her face. She rubs her concave stomach.

"Stop it," I say. "Smarten up. Where did you hear this nonsense?"

"It's in the Bible," says Catherine.

"Well, don't read the Bible," I tell her. "That's what Protestants do and look at them."

I did a poor job with Catherine, I know it. I didn't like to be there in the room with her.

Dr. Pat is waiting to talk to me.

"How'd it go?" he asks.

"Well, I'm no psychiatrist, I've discovered." I'm embarrassed. I peek around him, into the waiting room, where people sit wearing identical looks of annoyance.

"Will you keep trying?" he asks.

"I suppose."

He stands in front of me and gazes around. That glazed look the doctors sometimes get in moments of stillness. He sighs.

"I'm going to release her. If the parents won't let us send her up to Halifax there's not much we can do. Next week she'll faint in school again, we'll put her on IV and on and on it goes." Dr. Pat's eyes do a lazy sweep across the corridor and then land on me again. "Maybe you'll talk to her parents?"

I'm starting to wish he'd leave me alone. What I do is, I sit with old ladies and pat their hands.

Dr. Pat heads into Catherine's room to give the girl a final once-over before setting her free. I stand by the door. I see her lie there as he picks up her hand, turns her arm around to check the IV. She watches him take the stethoscope from his pocket, uses her free hand to pull aside her gown, offer him what's left of her chest.

SYLVIA'S HUSBAND IS called Ducky. They'd like me to call him Ducky. I try calling him Mr. Embree a couple of times but they won't let me get away with it.

"He's just old Ducky, Sister—that's what he answers to."

"Just call me Ducky," says Ducky, head bobbing.

I didn't know about Ducky, am surprised by Ducky. He works in the sawmills, and so disappears into the woods for most of the summer. Now it's fall and therefore he's back.

Sylvia wears a ring, but I assumed her husband was dead. I don't know why I assumed that. I think I must have believed that Sylvia is older than she is because of the way she looks. But look at Ducky—a woodsman, a good six feet to him, grey but nowhere near retirement. He infects us with his good health. Sylvia glows in his presence, and I keep ducking, flinching, imagining he's going to knock me over somehow.

He tries to dance with Sylvia, who is bedridden. "No, just watch," he says over our protests. He picks up her flaccid, see-through hands in his. My instinct is to call on Dr. Pat or someone.

But Ducky just begins to dance by himself, holding Sylvia's hands. He hums "In the Mood," closing his eyes. Manages to raise one of Sylvia's arms high enough so that he can even twirl himself underneath it, crouching low, almost going down on his knees and looking foolish. Sylvia wheezes laughter. Ducky lets one of her hands drop, and reaches his out toward me.

"How about it, Sister?"

Size of a baseball mitt.

Now that it's fall, Ducky visits every day. He's there during visiting hours, when I am. I still poke my head in the door, but there's only one chair in Sylvia's room. Or maybe there's two or three but with Ducky in there it hardly matters. He takes everything up. Sylvia waves to me, like a girl from a car window.

FALL GIVES ME the worst kind of dreams. All colour and sick sunlight. Crabapples rotting under trees, being reclaimed. I wait for Catherine to come back. Two weeks is all it takes.

She's grey. "You look like death," I tell her.

"I feel beatific," she says.

"Well, that's a hundred-dollar word."

"That's how I feel. I am shining my love out into the world."

"My goodness."

"Don't make fun of me," she says.

I'm startled. I have been imagining this whole time that she was making fun of me. I assumed we were speaking to each other in the same way my sisters and I always did—the hostility frothing up around the edges of our every sentence like scum on soup. We could spend entire holidays in a single house together, talking to each other like that, without a second thought, like picking and picking at your cuticles and being surprised when they start to ache and bleed.

We sit in dull silence for a moment or two.

"Can you bring me communion sometime?" Catherine asks.

"Would you take it?" I say, surprised again.

"Of course I would take it. It's all I would take. The Body. I will have the Body."

Well, I'm thinking, maybe we could sneak some peanut butter on there or some such thing.

"There's a priest who makes the rounds," I tell her. "I can bring him this week."

Catherine makes a face and writhes bonily under her sheet. "He's old!" she protests. "I don't want him."

It's difficult to hide my exasperation but I do because won't Hilary eat her hat if I'm the one to get this girl to swallow something of her own accord. Dr. Pat will wonder what they're paying her for.

"Well, you know I can't do it, Catherine," I say.

"Will you be there at least?"

My. I blink down at her. Am I touched?

"Of course," I tell her.

"Will the doctor be there?"

What to say about that? I suppose he will, if I tell him what's happening.

"What do you need the doctor for, to check your pulse?" I joke. "You plan on keeling over?"

"Don't make fun of me!" she yells.

I hurry down the hallway to find him, but run into Hilary instead. She stops dead in her tracks because, I realize, I'm smiling at her. Differently than I did in the office, I assume. She unruffles herself and cocks her head at me like a bird.

"She's going to eat something," I blurt.

Hilary blinks and blinks.

"She's going to take communion."

"Kah," says Hilary.

"Communion. The sacrament."

She keeps her bird-expression for a while. Bird-flown-into-a-window. Finally: "Oh," and exhales. "It's not much," she adds.

"Well, I was thinking we could..." I look down and witness my hands darting around in front of me. "Bulk it up somehow."

Hilary nods slowly, the fluorescent lighting playing across her wiry red hair. "Sister," she begins. No more blinking. "It's a very good start. But of course you see the problem. Again, it's all about religion for her. It's symbolic. It's not about eating."

"Well, it is, because she'll actually be eating something."

"Yes of course, but we're, we're, what we're trying to do is break down some of these psychological barriers. It has to mean something when she takes a bite — to Catherine. It has to mean she wants to eat. Do you see what I mean? It can't just mean more of the same thing — I want God, I want God, I don't want food. She has to want food, you see? For food's sake."

"For food's sake," I repeat, hands still.

She nods, smiles. I smile as well.

"Well, I think we should ask the doctor," I say as I move around Hilary. She follows me to his office without a word.

In a moment of what I am certain must have been boredom, Catherine once asked me why I became a nun. I asked did she want the long version or the short version.

"Short version," the thing replied. Not a moment's hesitation.

The short version was this. I was nineteen and sitting having a beer in the sun with my friend Dell Mercer. She was not my best friend or even a particularly good friend, but more one of those inevitable friends—someone you've known since preschool who is as much of a fixture in your life as a parent or a pet. In fact I remember it was Grade two when Dell decided she wanted people to call her Dell instead of Adela. I was the reason. She thought it sounded too much like my name. But was she sorry by Grade Three, because everyone started chanting "The Farmer in the Dell" at her in the playground, and I think she blamed me for it right up until Grade Seven or so.

But since this was the short version, I didn't tell Catherine all that.

I just told her I was nineteen and sitting having a beer in the sun with my friend Dell Mercer. It was summer and we were both home from school—she nursing, me teaching. We were in her parents' backyard overlooking the wharf, watching tourists bob around in their sailboats, and she announced she was getting married. I squealed and pretended to fumble my beer and did and said all the things girls are supposed to on these occasions. Of course I asked to see her ring.

Dell told me, "We haven't got it yet. Terry's got to save up for a while. I want a real rock. I've always had nice things, and you only get married once, so I feel like I deserve a real rock. I've waited a long time to get married. So I told him, Terry, I want a rock. Nothing else will stand."

She kept saying, rock. A real rock, over and over. Beer in the sun, sun on the water, water under sailboats. I thought *I think I'll be a nun* after that.

Catherine of course could be counted upon to find this story idiotic.

I didn't tell her my secret reason. The other, the story of the rock, was my official reason, and it's true that Dell going on and on like that very much clinched the deal for me. But there was another story I'd never tell Catherine. It happened when I was her age, wandering around in the fields at my grandparents' place in Margaree. It was summer then also, but late, long-shadowed and hot. No ocean nearby with a breeze off the water to cool things off. The high grass had turned gold, dead from heat. I was listening to the silence, the strange hot buzz of nothing — just sky and dry grass. I bumped against a stinking willie, which nodded at me, and as I passed I glimpsed an enormous bumblebee nodding along with it. I jumped — I'd had a terror of bees ever since one of my stupider brothers took to a hive with a rake. But the big bee wasn't perturbed. It just rode the nodding flower, not budging or moving its wings. I bent over and nudged the stinking willy again, ready to run. The bee still didn't move. I must have watched it forever before finally extending a finger and actually poking the bee. Nothing. It was frozen, somehow.

And then, panic. Like the world had stopped, and the hot buzz of nothing in every direction.

Something like, *Help me i'm alone.*

"BODY OF CHRIST."

Dr. Pat just stands there. I catch his eye over the priest's shoulder and mouth a big *amen.*

"Oh!" exclaims Dr. Pat. "Amen." The priest gazes at

him with indulgence, raises the host mouth-level. Dr. Pat stares at it. Oh, I am going to start laughing if someone doesn't do something.

"Open your mouth to receive the host," encourages the priest in church tones.

Dr. Pat appears horrified, and I must say it unnerves me as well, the idea of him standing before the priest just opening his mouth like the rest of us, waiting. Him not even Catholic, but a doctor. We didn't tell the priest because Catherine was so insistent—Dr. Pat had to receive too, or else she wouldn't. Guilt. My fingertips tingle, my palms seep with it. And I keep wanting to laugh.

I only wish Catherine had insisted on Hilary receiving as well. Hilary is the one who needs to be here with her mouth hanging open. She would know the responses, the amens, when to stand and when to kneel. She would know it like a baby knows to suck, and be infuriated. Thanks be to God. The words would fly from her mouth, her mouth would hang open, her tongue would pop out of its own accord, welcoming the host. Not a thing the social worker could do about it. She knows, and that's why she hasn't come. "I want nothing to do with this," she said in Dr. Pat's office. Her face went red to match her hair. She's very cool, Hilary, but her face betrays her. If it weren't for that fair complexion and those telltale blotches that say *I would like to choke you, Sister Anita*, you'd suppose butter wouldn't melt in her mouth.

Dr. Pat kept yanking on his telephone cord in the face of Hilary's reproach. He held it with both hands and kept pulling the curls apart and then gently letting them sproing together again. For a moment I thought he was going to start chewing on the thing.

"I just want to make sure we're doing everything we can," he said to the cord. "I want to leave no stone unturned—for Catherine's sake."

"Then have her committed," said Hilary. "Send her to Halifax. Get her the professional care that she needs, don't participate in this fantasy."

"Pardon me?" I said.

"Her fantasy," repeated Hilary. "The thing that is making her sick."

I decided I didn't need to answer. I just sat back in my chair, relaxing.

"Catherine is running this," said Hilary. "She's—she's in the director's chair."

I tittered then, Hilary's blotches deepening. I don't know why. Catherine in her nightdress shouting *Action!*

"Body of Christ," to me. Open your mouth and close your eyes.

Then he turns to Catherine. She gets to stay in bed.

"Body of Christ."

"Amen." Catherine sticks her tongue out. It's as white as the host itself. White as the blood of the lamb and all that.

And it's over already. As the priest blows out the communion candle, we all watch Catherine close her mouth and swallow. I suppose it's a bit anticlimactic. He turns to shake hands with Dr. Pat, and then there is a noise—a big one. We all twitch and look at each other for explanation before we think to look at Catherine again. She's sitting there with a face of mild surprise, hands lightly resting on her stomach. It makes the noise again, but louder.

"There's a demon down there," she remarks.

"It certainly sounds like it," admits Dr. Pat. He moves toward her, reaching for his stethoscope. But she grabs his hand before it gets to his pocket. She grabs it and places it on her belly.

"Feel," she tells him.

And he does, he stands there feeling. I want to snap at him to cut it out, and I look around for the priest, who is mumbling dazedly to himself in the corner, packing away his communion things. Old. As Catherine has already pointed out.

"I'm going to be sick," she announces, and starts to clamber out of bed. Whereupon of course she collapses. Dr. Pat must pick her up. Dr. Pat gathers her into his arms like kindling.

And for God's sake, her gown has not been tied in the back and now it slips right off the creature, skin melting off bones. The poor priest is a white-robed dervish, whirling from the darkened room.

IT OCCURS TO me that I haven't visited Sylvia in a while and she is probably wondering what's gotten into me. Well, Sylvia, I will tell her. I just got so wrapped up in that little girl down the hall. Yes — the one who doesn't eat. Wouldn't swallow her own spit if she had her druthers. Would want to know how many calories it had in it. Well, baby steps, Sylvia. We got her to take the host, and that's a beginning, now, isn't it? You could do a lot worse now, couldn't you, Sylvia, than the Body of Christ? I'll say.

And we will laugh quietly — Sylvia wheezily — at my near-irreverence. Sylvia enjoys those kind of jokes, the ones that take a run at blasphemy, swerving away at the last dangerous moment, like kids playing chicken.

Sylvia's room is darkened too — maybe everyone on the floor is taking communion today, the traumatized priest shambling from room to room: *B-b-b-body of Christ. B-body. Body.* Stuffing the wafer distractedly down everyone's throat. *Take this and eat it.*

I will tell the story to Sylvia sometime. Not today, but when I'm feeling a bit more collected and can joke about the hapless Dr. Pat and the muttering priest. Sylvia will enjoy hearing me make fun of the priest and the doctor, the men she depends on to such an unthinkable extent. I imagine you have to hate them a little. Need to see them ridiculed at times — it brings relief. I can do that for Sylvia.

But Ducky's in there and the room is hazy, rank. His flannelled back is to me, a third wall, and from behind it come low, private giggles. Surreptitious wheezings. Snatches of song from Ducky.

Yooooo doooooo
something
to me

He is hamming up the Yooooo dooooo's, drawing them out forever. Sylvia coughs voluptuously and Ducky turns his head in a deliberate, aristocratic sort of gesture. A gesture that plays at luxury and indulgence. I see his blunt woodsman's profile outlined in the dark—the scar that dents his cheek.

Yoooooooo dooooooooo.

Here is what he's doing. He's inhaling, and then letting the smoke pour out as he sings. It cascades from his face and swirls heavenward, enveloping them both as he extends the cigarette to his wife. A more honest gesture, now, a gesture like the nurses when they feed her, only loving.

And then of course he takes a look around, a guilty boy. As he has probably been doing intermittently throughout this performance.

And if they think I am going to stand here denouncing this and that, they are not smart. If they think I'm going to slap my palm against the light switch and start hollering for doctors and nurses and the pope, they don't have to concern themselves. If they suppose I could possibly bother with any such nonsense, let them turn around and get on with what they're doing. Let them do as they please, the whole bunch of them. Eat and smoke and starve and stand on your head as far as I'm concerned. Live and die and do what you want all over the place. I won't be the one to say a word.

AN OTHERWORLD

AN OTHERWORLD

Falling down the stairs, Erin's only thought was: *God damn Sean!* Because she knew he would take this as proof that he'd been right about her bicycle accident three months ago, which proved she had some kind of a psychological problem.

You hurt yourself when you're upset about something, Sean had said.

There was a speed bump, she repeated at him. On the bike path. On the hill! It wasn't even marked.

I went to get your bike, said Sean, and there was a big sign. Speed bump, it said.

There was no sign!

There was a sign.

I am calling the city, Erin said, and I'm going to complain that there wasn't a sign.

There was a sign, said Sean. Go check.

Without telling him, once the black eyes from her broken nose had dwindled to under-eye smudges and people no longer gave her appalled looks when she appeared on the street, she slipped into the river valley to visit the scene of the accident. Just walking down the same hill made her stomach roil—provoked a visceral remembrance of sailing over her handlebars during the long, doomed *oh-no* time warp that hitting the speed bump had triggered. She had been playing a lot of computer games that month and, after crunching face-first to the ground, her instinct was to wonder: *When did I last hit save? I can go back.* It was that feeling of losing, of having screwed up badly in the game and just wanting to quit in disgust and start over.

Then she stood up. No problem. Bounced to her feet. *I'm okay*, she thought, *I'm fine.* Blood started getting everywhere at that point and an over-tanned man who'd been leaving the pitch-and-putt with his preteen daughter reparked his car and rushed over to offer assistance, the grossed-out twelve-year-old wincing in his wake.

In the stairwell, she landed against her outstretched hand, the same hand she had outstretched to slow herself down after having flown over the handlebars, the hand with all the subsequent soft tissue damage, which had kept her from doing yoga for three months and was only now starting to get better.

Motherfucker, said Erin in the stairwell—the word echoed in noisy layers. She took advantage of the privacy and crumpled up there for a while, cradling her hand.

Then she bounced to her feet just the same way she had on the bike path, put her shoe back on and finished moaning quickly. She was already late for the welcome reception.

Everyone except Erin had arrived by the time she got there, and her dad waggled his eyebrows at her, faux-jocular. He extended his arm, the better to herd her toward his new accountant and also new best friend and business partner, Frank. Blank-minded and smiling, Erin held out her freshly damaged hand to Frank and next she was shrieking on her knees as Frank staggered backward, staring at his palm as if it pulsed with electricity.

Motherfucker, Erin said again. It was something she didn't often say in front of her parents. Cock, shouted Erin. Sean rushed to pick her up and sit her down somewhere.

THE STAIRWELL, SHE said to Sean back in their room, was very poorly lit.

Don't even start that, Erin, said Sean.

No, I'm just saying, putting aside your theory for a minute, a person can't really see where they're going in there.

Especially when a person is hurling herself down the stairs.

They were in Belize. They were at this ridiculous resort on Ambergris Caye. Nobody else was at the resort except for the wedding party, even though the place was huge. If not for the resort staff, it would feel like some kind of post-apocalyptic celebration—all other humans vaporized. They had it to themselves because Frank was the owner and because it was off-season, and because her father was Frank's biggest investor.

Did you notice, she said to Sean, how Frank wears a

diamond in either ear? He looks like a lunatic.

He is a lunatic, agreed Sean, allowing her to change the subject. Talk to him. Whole other planet. Did you talk to him?

No, said Erin. I didn't get a chance to talk to him after he hurt me.

Which was a stupid thing to say because it led them directly back to the topic at hand.

This was Erin, Sean had come to understand. This was what Erin did. Help me; get away from me; ow that hurt; come here.

SEAN DIDN'T THINK it was that she didn't want to be getting married to him. He had his theories, but he didn't think that was it. He thought it could be attributed to how her father was running the wedding like one of his golf weekends, and also relationship issues leftover from Ames.

Ames was the man with whom Erin had spent her twenties "being hippies together," as she described it. It had been such an obvious move of rebellion against her father it was embarrassing—Erin herself said that. Listening to Erin talk about her past, you would think she was the most self-aware person on the planet. Which is to say, not someone prone to hurling herself down flights of stairs and blaming it on the lighting. So she and Ames lived in a cabin on the Sunshine Coast, grew vegetables and kept bees. They weren't dropouts, they told themselves, dropping out was negative, a turning away, and this was a turning toward. They wanted to live authentically, like

Henry David Thoreau, whom Ames was very into. Ames kept journals like Thoreau did, and made money working up and down the coast doing carpentry for his fellow authentic-livers, often getting paid in loaves of bread and baskets of blackberries that he could have picked himself in about twenty minutes basically anywhere on the coast.

He called himself a "woodworker," never a carpenter. This was Erin's scornful joke. She'd had a lot of grim fun, in the two years Sean had known her, at Ames's expense. Erin told Sean that, authentic living aside, Ames had nurtured ambitions to be an actor. Ha ha. He thought Hollywood was bullshit, as you do, but great acting, like woodworking, was a marriage of craft and art. Ha. And, okay, the truth was, acting was not an entirely unreasonable ambition for Ames. He was, Erin admitted, "beautiful," all rangy limbs and the obligatory mid-nineties shaggy dishabille, a look that still made Erin a little giddy, like when she came across old photos of Kurt Cobain or the Soundgarden guy. Every once in a while Ames would take the ferry to Vancouver to audition for something or another, but all he got was extra work and the occasional gay come-on. Gays loved Ames, confided Erin. I mean, of course they're going to love a good-looking guy, but there was something about Ames, they just *adored* him.

It went to Ames's head, long story short. He finally met, claimed Erin, one too many people who just *adored* him. There was an agent who promised to get him modelling work, and actually accomplished this. Ames returned to the coast one day with a pair of $400 sunglasses holding back his hair.

We have to move the hives, Erin told him, the bear is back.

God, said Ames, removing the sunglasses and gathering his hair into a ponytail at the back of his skull. It was a gesture meant to get across great depths of torment. I can't deal with the *hives* anymore. I mean, Jesus, Erin. As if the hives were her fault.

Then Ames sat Erin down and described all the ways he had become unhappy with her.

It was embarrassing because of how Erin had renounced everything for Ames and his sinews and the vegetables and bees and their lame voluntary-simplicity cliché. Erin remembered being twenty-two and telling her father she pitied him in response to his telling her she was being slutty and throwing her life away. Then her father decided to say what he did, and she said what she said in response. It was one of those detonator moments—a conversation that implodes time and space and opens up a kind of portal, like in video games. You pick up a coin or open a chest; you say the right thing, or say the wrong thing. And next thing you know the world around you shudders and gives way, depositing you into a completely new dimension, an otherworld.

What happened was that Erin's father, Ron, decided to impart to his daughter the axiom about no one wanting to buy a cow that gives its milk away for free.

Maybe, Erin told him—vibrating like a kettle on the boil—maybe the cow just wants to get milked.

You have to know Erin's family to understand how a comment like this would land.

You are never going to understand anything about real life, Erin told her father in the strangled, white-lipped silence that followed. It was a silence that would endure and thicken between them for the next five years—that was the portal she had tipped them into. The portal to a silent world. You are so caught up in your traditionalist dogmas, she said to dumbstruck Ron.

Tra-*dish*-onalist *dawg*-mas, Erin said to Sean, that was my big phrase back then. I thought it was just so clever. When Erin described herself saying things like this now, she did it as a parody. She adopted her "lumpy gran-ola" voice, a grating singsong delivery, nasal with self-righteousness—as if every sentence she uttered should end with an emphatic "man" or "dude." Sean found it a little ruthless. Stop it, he laughed. You can't beat yourself up for being young.

You weren't being an idiot when you were in your twenties, Erin accused.

I was being my own special kind of idiot, answered Sean. In fact, at the start of his twenties, Sean worked at a UPS call centre that had opened the very spring he graduated from university, and counted himself lucky. He banked his paycheques and rented a studio apartment in a concrete high-rise and took the bus to work. He applied for promotions within the company and bought mutual funds and had his first house by the time he was twenty-six, just in time to get married to a woman from his office to whom he now referred by no other name except "The Beast." Later, after he divorced and went back to school, he met people like Erin, people who structured their twenties around snowboarding trips and the obtainment and usage of pot and had gone to Burning Man and had multiple sex partners and had taught in Japan and volunteered in Africa and sailed in sailboats around the Gulf Islands, and that's when he started feeling like his own special kind of idiot. Now he was forty-two.

By their second year of living together, Sean was spending every weekend tricking out their basement dungeon. It was his engagement present to Erin. But from the moment he set it up, he found the busywork of tinkering around down there gave him almost as much pleasure as the purpose it was intended for. He liked puttering and experimenting in his time off, looking up stuff online, inventing new things for them to try. Erin started calling it Satan's Workshop. He'd ordered plans for bondage furniture and so far had built his own whipping chair, and he'd also bought an old church confessional pew from the antique mall and sanded and stained it, drilled holes and added hooks and straps and turned it into a kind of sicko kneeling structure which Erin, with her Catholic background, loved. Now he'd moved on to a Saint Andrew's Cross, which was the biggest thing he'd ever done. He'd held off on this project for a while because the dungeon had metastasized to such a degree after Erin moved in, and was getting harder to pack up whenever they had friends over wanting their inevitable tour of the house. The last time Erin's parents had come to visit, it had taken all weekend to find a hiding place for everything. Her father had insisted on seeing Sean's "workshop" and then laughed at Sean as he looked around at the pristine tools hanging on their hooks.

This place is immaculate, Ron said. Give me a break, please, Sean. You don't so much as lift a hammer down here.

Sean had no idea what he would do with the Saint Andrew's Cross when the time came. Likely he would just end up throwing a tarp over it and hoping no one got curious.

DID YOU AND Ames ever do this kind of stuff? Sean wanted to know after Erin moved in.

Ames and I had twenty-something sex, she said. Where you do it constantly and think you must be having a blast.

You weren't enjoying it? You don't have to say that, you know.

You think you're enjoying it, said Erin. There isn't a lot of difference, at that age, between thinking you're enjoying something and actually enjoying it.

Then how do you know the difference? said Sean.

You know later, once you're *really* enjoying it.

Then how do you know you're ever *really* enjoying it? They were lying in bed, having one of the lazy, pointless conversations of which they had so many early in their relationship. Where the actual subject under discussion didn't matter because all they really wanted was to feel each other's voices buzzing in their bodies.

How do you know you don't still just think you are enjoying it? said Sean. Like right now?

Because of having an orgasm, said Erin.

But, come on. You had orgasms!

Erin stretched then, sending her limbs in all directions like the da Vinci drawing. I didn't even know what an orgasm *was* in those days.

Sean understood she wasn't being literal. He knew he was paying more attention to the conversation than Erin was; than it really merited. But he wondered: Is this a compliment? Or what is it?

OKAY, STOP STOP stop, said Erin. They were celebrating one year of being engaged and it was their first time using the basement in a serious way. Sean could tell that she meant it. They didn't have a safe word, because that made it seem too hardcore. Too much like people who dressed up in masks and rubber, who said mean things to each other, like in movies.

Mother*fucker*, said Erin. Whoo.

Sean looked at the cane in his hand. I didn't do it hard, like at all, he said.

Whoo. It really hurt, said Erin.

They had just bought it. Erin read about it online. It was fancy and expensive—rattan with a leather grip. Sean had offered to slap together something similar in his workshop, but Erin said it couldn't just be some stick from out in the yard; it had to be rattan.

But I thought—

Ha ha, yes I know, said Erin. But it *really* hurts.

It should only hurt a little bit? This alarmed Sean, because it contradicted the rules as he understood them up until now.

No, said Erin. It should hurt. But it shouldn't *really* hurt.

This made Sean think back to their conversation in bed in the early days of their relationship. Really versus not really.

Let me up, said Erin, becoming restless. I have to pee, sweetie.

ERIN WENT FOR a walk by herself along the beach the morning of the wedding. Frank's two dogs, a pair of excitable, flap-eared mutts who had the run of the resort, came with her uninvited. They were the happiest dogs in the world, it seemed—they couldn't believe their luck, living here on the beach with Frank, meeting new people all the time, having each other to play with. They managed to accompany Erin and play frantically with one another throughout her entire walk. It was not as peaceful and meditative as she'd intended it to be. The dark one would chase the light one, then the light one would whip around and they would face off, crouching in the dried seaweed, communicating with lolling tongues. The next instant, the light would be after the dark. They'd jump in the surf, cool off, splash, pretend to bite one another. Then they'd notice Erin had gone a bit farther down the beach than they preferred her to be, and would run to catch up.

You guys are exhausting, Erin said.

Approaching the resort, she ran into Frank. Erin and Frank hadn't warmed to one another at the reception the night before as a result of Frank crushing her hand. He'd steered clear of her the rest of the evening.

There she is, said Frank now. They were the only two people on the beach. Our child-bride.

Erin was thirty-eight. Hi, she said.

Frank was as bald as a stump and the size of the diamonds in his ears really did make him look crazy. He looked like a big bald infant wearing lady's jewellery. The dogs were overjoyed to see him and capered, whining, about his shins.

How are you liking the place? Frank wanted to know, waving his arms down around his knees to make sporadic contact with the dogs.

It's beautiful, said Erin. And it was, kind of. But she was coming to believe she wasn't a Caribbean sort of person. It all looked great from a distance but the turquoise ocean turned out to be warm as urine and when she got in it her eyes and mouth burned with salt. Also the white sand made her impatient. She found it hard to believe it wasn't artificial — silicone or something. She was tempted to ask Frank if they manufactured it somewhere and had it shipped in, but when she'd mentioned this possibility to Sean the night before he'd laughed until he couldn't breathe.

You have to be honest with me now, said Frank, spreading his arms toward the ocean. Does it get any better than this?

No, said Erin. It doesn't.

Frank stooped to palm a coconut and the dogs went even crazier, perhaps thinking he was going to throw it for them, or maybe just because he'd put his face, momentarily, at their level.

Your opinion as a bride is very valuable, Frank told her, frowning as he straightened, either to indicate sudden seriousness or else back pain. So I appreciate hearing that. I plan on weddings being the engine that makes this little operation run. And it's all about making the bride happy, after all.

I think people will love it, Erin told him, which was not a lie. She didn't love a lot of the things everybody else seemed to love. She used to think that had to mean other people were wrong. But she didn't believe that anymore, Erin realized—at some point she'd stopped assuming she was right and everyone else was wrong. Now she figured she was likely as wrong as the next person. But Frank took her statement kindly and beamed his stumpy sunburned pleasure at her, diamonds sparkling on either side of his head. He held the coconut aloft.

I will plant this for you, Frank declared. The first bride to grace our Caye. He began to clamber up a dune in search of an appropriate tree-planting spot as the dogs freaked out at his feet.

We'll call it—I'm so sorry, what's your name again, dear?

Erin, said Erin.

We'll call this "Erin's Tree," announced Frank.

She watched as he negotiated another dune and then, for no obvious reason, fell over into the sand.

The dogs went mad and leapt upon him.

Oh my God, said Erin, darting forward, holding her arms out as if to pick him up.

Frank writhed in the fake white sand, fending off the

ecstatic dogs, who licked him as if he'd dropped to ground precisely to give them this opportunity. With gratitude and abandon.

I'm all right, Frank assured her. I have a bad hip. It just gives out sometimes—poof.

But Erin could see the reality of pain in Frank's face, there was real pain there now, clouding up the sunny madness, pain the dogs were doing their best to lick away. Frank's hat had been knocked from his head and he lay there, bald and bejewelled, looking more like a helpless infant than ever.

ERIN WENT BACK to the hotel room to find Sean and see if she could talk him into a quick pre-wedding spanking. He'd refused to raise a hand to her since they arrived, for fear a chambermaid or relative would overhear and get the wrong idea. I need you to spank the weird out of this place for me, she told him.

Sean said he was too self-conscious. The walls were like onion skin.

So Erin went for a swim and five minutes into it came face to face with a small stingray. She'd petted one when they'd gone snorkelling a couple days ago, but that time the guide had been holding it still for her.

And clambering up onto the dock to escape the stingray, she tore her thigh open on a spike. What was the spike doing there? It was errant, poking out at an impractical angle, and the only such spike on the dock, but Erin had found it.

Sнe didn't end up needing stitches but Sean told her, a few minutes before they got married, that maybe to be on the safe side they should ask one of the waiters to strap her to a trolley and wheel her down the aisle.

I like the being strapped down part, she joked back. Do I get to pick my own waiter?

She decided not to let Sean know how angry the comment had made her. At this point, she just wanted to limp down the fucking aisle, say the stupid vows and get drunk and then get on a plane home so they could be together in the way they always were. Belize was a mistake. Accepting the resort package as her father's wedding gift—which had made her feel so mature at the time, so above it all, so water-under-the-bridge—was a mistake. It had become a TV wedding. The waving palm tree fantasy of some fourteen-year-old daddy's-little-princess.

She'd been kidding herself. She thought this as she kissed Sean at the reception, after everyone began tinking their forks against their glasses at them for what had to be the twenty-seventh time. She hadn't exited the field of battle with her father. She'd surrendered.

Sean got divorced at a Starbucks. He and The Beast met every week at the Starbucks at the West Edmonton Mall, the biggest mall in North America. They had a DIY divorce because Sean was still, at the time, his own special kind of idiot. Why not part amicably, he thought. There was no need for a lawyer—a lawyer was cold and impersonal, a lawyer would introduce an unnecessary adversarial element to the proceedings and why do that? Hadn't they had enough of being adversaries? Good faith, therefore. Plus it wouldn't be fair, because he could afford a lawyer and The Beast could not. So he and The Beast hashed a deal out together, at Starbucks, using documents from the internet. She drank Frappuccinos and he drank whatever the featured brew happened to be that day.

The Beast was unemployed except for the knitting lessons she gave and the crafts she sold every summer at the farmers' market and online. She came up with some impressive stuff—The Beast could knit food, perfectly recognizable olives and hamburgers and ice cream cones. Years ago, he had encouraged her in this; he made good money at UPS, so why shouldn't she follow her dreams, quit her soul-killing administrative job and knit food all day?

And now, therefore, it was his fault she had been out of the workforce for so long. Out of guilt, and a desperation to get away, he gave her everything.

DON'T BE so hard on yourself, Erin told him, on the plane back to Canada. It seemed like there was no other way of dealing with the terrible wedding on the fake white sand against the swimming-pool ocean, not to mention their hangovers, but to talk about how terrible their previous relationships had been.

They'd heard each other's stories many times before. They always ended up, these stories, with one of them telling the other: Don't be so hard on yourself.

But you guys weren't miserable, argued Sean. You and Ames. You didn't cohabit in complete and utter misery for ten years and just, like, stick with it because you figured it was the right thing to do. You stayed together because you were happy. And then you broke up once you weren't happy anymore, like reasonable human beings.

No, said Erin.

Yes, said Sean, who had heard about it enough to feel comfortable contradicting her. Ames just came home one day and said he wasn't happy.

Yes, said Erin. But it doesn't mean we were happy right up until that exact point.

Well, that's kind of how you've always described it.

Erin looked past Sean out the window. It showed a wall of cloud the colour of cement.

But I knew that he resented me, she said. For a long time. I just didn't know what to do about it. And when he came home that day with the sunglasses, one of the things he said made him mad was how I resented his acting career. And I couldn't figure that out, because I was the one who helped him get his resumé and headshot online, I was the one who found him an extras agent. I was always trying to find him work. So I didn't understand what he was saying. And it wasn't until quite a few months after he moved out that I got it. He wasn't mad because I resented his career, he was mad because I was the thing that wasn't his career—I was the anti-career. So he couldn't imagine me doing anything but resenting it. I was the thing on the other side of the ferry crossing that had nothing to do with what he wanted anymore.

Sean was beginning to fall asleep. He'd made the mistake of thinking this was another one of their lazy conversations.

But you guys were happy, he insisted with his eyes closed. Up until then.

I was, said Erin. I was the one who was happy.

She seemed to sneeze in slow motion into her hands. Sean opened his eyes and sat up. The whole time he had known Erin, she had never done this. She wasn't a crier.

It's just this whole past week, she told him. The wedding with all the family and everything.

But it's over, said Sean. He put his arms around her.

When we get home, Erin whispered after a moment, I want you to beat the living shit out of me.

They'd never gone a week without before.

CLEAR SKIES

CLEAR SKIES

People were laughing, afterwards. They laughed during, too, before anyone knew what was going on or what might happen. The thing to do upon landing was tell the story and make jokes. When Sara was up there, seconds after the *boom*, she imagined doing just that. She'd even rehearsed it a bit for future audiences.

I was so scared. I thought an engine had exploded. I thought: well, this is it.

At the airport, Terry was carrying a copy of Sara's book for identification purposes. She saw him from a distance, peering down at the author's photo every time a new arrival emerged through the sliding doors. His eyes went from her face on the book, to her face in real life, and still they passed right by her. She had to come and tap him on the shoulder.

"It's me," she said, pointing to the book. It was her first book. The person in the photograph was nineteen years old. Sara's tap had surprised him and he gave her an instinctive, hostile look. "What a tiny airport!" she added.

"Oh!" yelled Terry, grabbing her hand. He asked how her flight had been.

"The plane was struck by lightning," Sara said. She told her little story for him, watched his blue eyes widen. It was a good way to kick things off.

They had to wait for Herb, the fiction guy, before making their way to the monastery, but his flight was not due for another twenty minutes. Sara went to the bathroom as Terry studied the back of Herb's book, which was stamped with a gilded reminder of his nomination for a major book award the previous year.

Everywhere she went in the airport, there were posters—on practically every wall. It was almost ridiculous, the number of posters. She saw such posters in her grocery store, and the post office. But here it was the same poster over and over again, the same pudgy, uncute face.

"What's with all the posters?" she asked Terry.

He jumped again at the sound of her voice. I will get a little bell to wear around the retreat, Sara decided.

"Oh," he said, looking around. "Marie." As if the girl in the posters were related to him or something, a colleague maybe. "She's been gone a month now. Everyone's desperate. *Sad*."

"But why —" Sara didn't know how to ask the question without sounding callous. "I mean—there's only one missing kid in the entire province?"

Terry shrugged. He was supposedly a playwright, but Sara had never seen any of his work. "It's one of those things—mysterious. You know, her parents are still together, so it's not like one of them nabbed her. Just disappeared out of the blue."

Sara felt what she knew was a prissy twinge of annoyance, because the phrase was inappropriate. You didn't disappear out of the blue. You *appeared* out of it, suddenly, like a holy bolt of lightning.

It was a year in the world where people seemed to be dying explosively or else disappearing without so much as a bleat. She wanted to leave it behind, which was why she'd said yes to the retreat. She'd liked the sound of it: *a prairie retreat*. The brochure Terry'd sent her showed photographs like abstract paintings: one thick, vertical band of brilliant green topped by a second, thicker band of glaring blue. *Your view*, the brochure promised.

On TV there was nothing but explosions anymore. In her city, in the past year, an abrupt slew of people had blanked from existence as if culled by hungry aliens. Pictures of people who had recently failed to exist were always on the front page of the paper. It was not like she ever bought the paper—front page after front page accosted her whenever she walked up and down the street. There was no avoiding anything.

She had a brother in Duncan who, like her, was no longer in the family. They argued on the phone. Wayne always seemed to think it was natural and okay for he himself to have left, but scandalous and obscene for her. Plus, he didn't mind the bombs. "It's about time they started bombing *something*," he opined. He called Sara a hippie, since he couldn't convincingly use words like *harlot* and *jezebel* now that they were equally damned.

They rolled along in Terry's big white van. The landscape was just like the abstract painting in the brochure,
only endless and on every side. Just when she was starting to feel panicky about it, hills appeared on either side
of the highway, and then they were descending into a pic-
turesque—there was no other word for it—valley. Terry
gestured to one of the hills, and she and Herb looked. A
crucifix loomed; a sprawling, one-storey building crouched
behind it as if for protection.

"There it is," said Terry.

"Oh *no*," said Sara.

Herb was sitting in the front seat. He had talked all the
way from the airport, which would have bothered her if
he wasn't so likeable and engaging. A publisher's dream—
that's the kind of writer Herb was. Now he turned and
flashed his teeth at her.

"Everything all right?"

In the rear-view mirror, Terry glanced and squinted.
He was thinking—*Ten days with this person, morning, noon
and night*—and so she laughed.

"I forgot about the *God* thing," she explained. "The
crucifix up there." She grimaced and shuddered comically
for them. Terry and Herb both knew about Sara—how she
had made her name. She had been briefly famous, as a teenager. They laughed and nodded.

THE FIRST MORNING of the retreat, her toilet backed up.
It was the worst thing that could happen. She had used it,
was the problem. She had used it right after breakfast.

She flushed the thing as many times as she dared before slinking to Terry's office. At the grim look on her face, he jerked himself to his feet and pulled the door shut — expecting maybe news of an unwanted grope from Herb, a veiled threat from a born-again student.

"No, no, nothing bad," Sara assured him. Cringing, she explained.

"We'll just call in the maintenance man," Terry told her, managing to wink and look jolly.

I shit, she had basically walked up to Terry and announced. *Hello, strange man. There is something I'd like you to know about me and here it is.* Sara floundered at the thought of the maintenance man. Would she have to encounter this maintenance man at any point? Look him in the eye afterward?

"I don't know what you were planning on doing this morning," said Terry. "The groups don't meet until after lunch. You could go for a little walk maybe, while he's working."

Sara had been planning on having a shower — she hadn't bothered when she arrived the night before. Her hair was pulled back tight and neat so that none of its greasy strands would be noted.

She went for a walk. She went to see the labyrinth. Last night Terry told them how much visitors enjoyed walking the labyrinth, and she and Herb and Betty, the poet, and Marguerite, the children's writer, were welcome to do the same. It helped the students move forward with their writing, he said. Helped them to commit, to let go of whatever might be holding them back. They carried some object into the labyrinth with them that was meant to represent their problem, their block. They meditated as they walked and once they got to the middle, left the object there on the makeshift pedestal. Sara had walked straight through the labyrinth, stepping over its stone borders, to examine the pile of crap left on the pedestal, while everyone else remained outside, as if in respect. There were pebbles and sticks and small birds' feathers—but also single earrings, grocery receipts and a tube of lip gloss.

Now she circled the labyrinth, feeling resentful of it, the way she felt resentful of the crucifix. Last night at dinner she had said that she didn't know much about Catholicism, but a labyrinth seemed, to her, sort of pagan for a monastery. She understood ritual was a big deal in the Catholic church—on the plane, Sara's seatmate had yanked a rosary out of her purse after the *boom*, closed her eyes, fingered it bead by bead, whispering frantically. Still it seemed wrong to her, like Terry had led them through the bush to a golden calf.

From the opposite end of the table, Marguerite the children's writer contradicted her. She told Sara about the Catholic labyrinths at Chartres and Amiens, and how old they were, and Sara felt, as she often felt, the limits of her education. Still, she also felt like she was right and Marguerite was wrong. It was how she was raised. Christian or pagan, she wanted to say—pick one. It was like the photo in the brochure—a single slash of sky above a single slash of land.

When she returned to her room, a man was crouched over her toilet, cursing. She smoothed her hair and left without disturbing him.

AT LUNCH, THE instructors sat together shyly, having not had time to bond with their group members as yet, which it was clear they were expected to do. It seemed to Sara that Marguerite and Betty had the wrong jobs. Marguerite the children's writer was serious, highly educated and dressed in prim, greyish woolies despite the fact that it was August. She looked, in short, like a poet. Betty was twenty-eight and wore a black minidress and a clattery sequence of bangles on either wrist. You could see the children's writers yearned for Betty. Whereas the poets—many of whom had ten years or more on their mentor—raised eyebrows at each other every time the cafeteria shook with Betty's overloud laughter. This happened so much that Sara started to worry about Betty. Betty laughed at everything she—Betty—or anyone else, for that matter, said. It seemed compulsive after a while.

They spoke about the missing girl, Marie. Marguerite and Terry both lived in the province, and it seemed residents of the province could think of little else—just as people in Sara's city were preoccupied by the same phenomena, only in greater numbers. Here it was only Marie at the centre of the mystery. The mystery was Marie herself. In Sara's city the mystery was Absence—here Absence was Marie.

"Disappeared out of the blue," said Terry again. Betty laughed. Sara wondered if she had picked up on Terry's mistaken usage and was being indiscreet.

"Well—the weather has improved at least," remarked Marguerite.

Betty laughed, and then asked, "Sorry—was that a joke?"

Marguerite didn't smile, but rolled her eyes in a gesture, perhaps, of self-deprecation.

"No, I mean no more cloud cover," Marguerite explained. "Clear skies. It makes searching easier."

Sara glanced up, confused. "Why?" she said before she had time to think and stop herself. "Do they think she's up there somewhere?"

Betty laughed, vibrating the water in Sara's glass. At a table nearby, the poets drew themselves together.

"First of all," she said to her group after lunch. "I don't know what I'm doing here. You guys could just as well have applied to Herb's group. There is no difference between fiction and memoir as far as I'm concerned."

Nobody wanted to contradict her so early in the meeting, but she could see the scepticism behind their eyes. They were smiling at her but they were formulating objections.

"I mean, okay, what—right off the bat—what would you say is the difference between the two forms?"

Everyone knew, but no one wanted to say something so obvious. Also because it was clear Sara was planning to contradict the person who did. She waited them out until finally a woman her own age named Alison spoke.

"One's true, one's made up," Alison sighed.

"True, false; good, bad; black, white," Sara shot back— keyed up on nervous adrenalin and feeling as if she was barely making sense. "No. It's an imaginary distinction."

"But," the only man in the room leaned forward, brow pinching. He was in an awkward position already, and knew it. Even sitting down, he hulked over the women.

"But," the man repeated. His name was Mac. "Surely there are differences."

"No, there are no differences," Sara insisted. She didn't know why she was being so adamant—of course there were differences. Maybe it had to do with establishing authority—forcing them to agree to a patent untruth right off the bat. Two plus two is five, repeat after me.

"Even," persisted Mac, "attitudinally speaking. Attitudinally, wouldn't you have to take a completely different approach to writing a work of fiction than you would a personal memoir?"

Mac ducked his head and raised his eyes to her then. A gesture of deference that was almost dog-like.

Sara pretended to think about it but really she was trying to calm her nerves.

"But you are talking about," she said, "the kind of differences that exist between any two projects. I write . . . I want to write, say, a whimsical story from the point of view of a dog. The next day, I want to write some kind of—I don't know—something weighty. Something from the point of view of a, of a rape victim or something."

Everyone was suddenly watching her with their mouths shut. She glared back at them.

"There will always be attitudinal differences—from one story to the next—is what I'm saying," she continued, the jolt of annoyance having cleared her head. "My point is, they're all still going to be *stories*, no matter what category we choose to put them in—fiction or non."

Sara sat back in her chair, satisfied she had finally said

something teacherly, and ready to suggest a coffee break. But when she glanced at her watch she saw they had only been together in the meeting room for ten minutes or so. She suggested one anyway.

THE LAST TIME she spoke with her brother Wayne, he explained to her why it didn't matter that people were disappearing from the street. He said it was part of God's plan.

"I don't think it's part of God's plan," she replied.

"Well, what would *you* know about God's plan," said Wayne.

This is how they talked to each other. There were no particularly nuanced arguments, no fine points to be made.

"What do *you* know about God's plan," Sara jeered back at him.

"More than *you*," Wayne answered. Wayne had a blackboard in his apartment, Sara imagined, like a football coach would have. There was a line drawn down the middle in chalk. On one side of the blackboard was written *The Wayner* and on the other side, *Stupid Hippie*. And every time Wayne came back with a zinger like "more than *you*," a mark went under *The Wayner* and then he sat back, satisfied, licking the chalk from his fingers.

"It's God's *plan*," Sara exclaimed, like she was starting to understand. "I get it, I get it, the women are the chosen ones! It's been them all along! They've been called! They've left us all behind!"

Wayne sighed his disgust. "You pretend," he said, "to be stupid, and say stupid things when you know the truth as well as I do. I've never understood why you do that. It doesn't make you seem smart, if that's what you think."

"They're whores," said Sara. She stood and carried the phone with her to look out the window at her pansies.

"Yes."

"God is cleansing us of them."

"Yes."

"Just like the bombs. On the heathen cities. Right?"

"That's right."

"But *all* women on the outside are whores." Sara was babbling again, almost gleeful. "Yes? Right? And everyone outside Eden is a heathen. So why aren't we all disappearing? Why isn't the city burning around me? Where is the angry hand, reaching down to smite?"

She was leaning forward, grinning hard, as if Wayne were there in the apartment with her. But if Wayne were there, she knew she'd never talk like this.

He waited an insolent moment before answering.

"I left—and you know I left—because I didn't believe all that bullshit. I'm not a *fanatic*."

Shriek. She could almost hear the chalk against the board.

MAC CAME UP to her at the book table, where Sara was noting which of her books Terry had ordered to sell at the retreat. There were about twenty copies of her teenage memoir stacked there, and he had used it as a display copy too—*Escaping Eden*—the book that was to represent her as an author. Tucked behind the stack of memoirs were five copies of her second novel, and no copies of her first or her collection of stories.

She was standing there thinking that talking to her brother Wayne was like talking to God. Maybe this was the reason she still stayed in contact with Wayne, despite the futility of their conversations: the acid frustration it provoked. It was like talking to God—pointless, maddening and compulsive. Wayne didn't make sense; he didn't have to make sense. He didn't bow to the logic of Man. Wayne's wisdom was his unfathomable own—undreamt of in her philosophy. The Wayner was what The Wayner was.

"I loved it," Mac told her.

She swivelled and blinked. He smiled and reached to tap the stack of *Edens* with a hirsute finger.

"Oh—thanks, Mac."

"It's the reason I came here. I hope you don't—I mean I think you're a brilliant memoirist."

"Thanks," she said. They stared together at the pile of books. "Did you think I was going to be nineteen?"

"What?" said Mac.

"Everybody thinks I'm going to be nineteen. Because I was nineteen when I published the book, and it was such a big deal. Oh my God, she's nineteen! And they still make a big deal of it on the cover—see?" She picked up one of the copies, which was the newest edition, and showed him. She held the photo of the nineteen-year-old up beside her face.

Mac laughed a little. "I didn't think you'd be nineteen. But I did—you know, I read the book and I thought—I

want to learn from the person who wrote this book. I want
to tell my story with the same kind of honesty."

"I don't even remember writing it," Sara told him.

BETTY AND HERB were to read at the beginning of the
retreat, and she and Marguerite were to read at the end.
Herb, charismatic and engaging, was also a wonderful
reader, but his prize-winning book was about a middle-
aged male university professor having a torrid, forbidden
affair with one of his undergraduate female students. Sara
had read somewhere that the "twist" in Herb's novel, the
thing that elevated it from hackneyed smut, was the fact
that even though the sexual relationship starts out fuelled
by nothing but goatish lust (with the typical mid-life crisis
and dash of misogyny thrown in), it unexpectedly evolves
into a profound and tender love. Not even love *affair*,
but *love*. The couple take up arms, philosophically speaking, against their numerous inquisitors instead of slinking
away and apart as anyone would have expected. On the
contrary, they vigorously defend their love, repudiating
shame and defying censure—be it official or otherwise.
The review Sara read claimed this aspect of the novel was
what made it startling and brave. What made it brilliant,
the reviewer added, was that, for most of the novel, the
reader found herself taking the part of the inquisitors,
feeling the very same contempt and moral outrage, only
to be ambushed and chastened by the sudden purity of the
love story.

For this particular reading, however, Herb eschewed

the love story altogether in favour of the sex scenes. He strung them together, flipping from one marked page to the next so that the descriptions of the professor and student's couplings were relentless and all seemed to blur into one endless, gross encounter. Sara wondered if Herb was just getting a kick out of reading these words aloud in a monastery, out of the fact that celibate holy men slept and studied only a few feet away. Maybe he imagined his resonant stage-actor's voice carrying all the way into their wing, slipping like a tongue into hairy Franciscan ears.

She pictured her brother Wayne sitting in the back with his Chevron cap perched on the crown of his head, lips obliterated under his moustache, meaty arms folded.

Betty got up to read next. She wore a somewhat more revealing but less stretchy minidress than the one she'd been wearing all day, with long satin gloves and big crucifix earrings. She made some prefatory, self-deprecating jokes about herself and shrieked laughter into the microphone.

"This is a poem about my mother," she told everyone a moment later, wiping her eyes. She read the title—a sad, solemn title—and laughed again like it was a private, uproarious joke.

Betty did something to her voice for the reading—Sara had heard other poets do it too. Sometimes it seemed stagy and contrived and other times, depending on the poet, it worked well. With Betty it seemed natural. She changed her timbre substantially—the entire personality of her voice changed. It was low and meditative. There wasn't any laughter. It was the speaking-voice of Betty's mind.

Sara looked out the window and saw how the sunset

was painting the valley. Her eyes turned on like taps. She tried to get it under control. This happened at the movies sometimes—even during the previews. The music would swell, a camera would zoom in on a face, and it was as if someone had reached beneath her ribs and flicked a switch. It didn't matter what was going on, necessarily. The content wasn't the problem. It was a thing that happened outside of words.

Afterwards the polite thing to do was discuss the readings with Betty and Herb respectively.

"I *cried*," she told Betty, who looked startled, and then laughed. Sara laughed with her, feeling relief. This was the same sort of phenomenon as *my plane was hit by lightning*, the same sort of ritual. You speak it in defiance. It was freeing the same way blasphemy was freeing.

WHEN THEY WEREN'T having group meetings, they had private meetings, one on one. Individually, she found them to be splendid people, and wanted to assure them that the fact they had any proficiency at all was wonderful and they shouldn't get so tied up in knots about it because they also had jobs and houses and licences to drive cars, which made them like gods as far as Sara was concerned.

She and Mac conducted their meeting walking into town to buy alcohol and bottled water. It was coming toward the end of the week and people had started to sit outside and drink in the evenings, prompting Terry to bring his guitar out of his office and play Gordon Lightfoot songs.

Mac told her about his memoir as they walked the gash of road through the endless fields on either side. The sky felt like something they could disappear into. She made sure to walk in the middle of the road, like a child avoiding cracks in the sidewalk.

"This landscape is crazy!" Sara interrupted Mac at one point.

"Different from where *you* grew up," said Mac. Not a question. He figured he knew everything about her. He was, she had determined a few days ago, constantly angling to discuss *Eden*.

"I've never been to the Kootenays," he continued. "I love how you describe them in the book. The mountains and trees... the clouds against the mountains... 'yet another barrier.' It was great how... I mean, you said everything but the word 'prison,' right?"

"God-made dungeon," said Sara. She thought she was saying it spontaneously, but the moment she did, realized she had quoted the nineteen-year-old.

"Oh, that's right, that's right," said Mac. "You did say dungeon. But that sense of claustrophobia — it came across so well. None of that here, eh?" He gestured to the sky. Here you could gesture to the sky simply by raising your arms a few inches. "Nothing holding you back."

Sara was concerned because Mac was clearly modelling his book too closely on her own. His story wasn't even really his, but his grandfather's, who had been a leader in the Winnipeg General Strike. He had done endless research. He had, as he put it, "reams" of material.

She decided to tackle the subject head-on, to talk about

Eden as much as Mac craved in order to dissuade him, to
show how him wrong-headed it was. He wouldn't be able
to write his own book until he fell out of love with hers.

"Do you see why this approach can't work?" she demanded
as they walked. Walking made it easier to be honest, they
didn't have to look at each other. The crunch of gravel filled
in the conversational gaps. "The two books have nothing in
common."

"But it's more the *attitude* of your book I'm trying to
get at —"

"This attitude thing again —"

"The *tone*."

"The tone is internal, Mac. The tone is the inside of a
teenage girl's head. Do you think I had to go to the library
and research that?"

"But how did you . . . like that thing with the trees and
the mountains and the clouds against the mountains —
one barrier after another. Crafting those kinds of metaphors. That's the sort of thing I'm after."

"They weren't metaphors," said Sara. "That was how
things looked, through my eyeballs, and so I wrote it
down."

Crunch gravel, crunch gravel. Mac was casting a
shadow over her. He is so *big*, thought Sara. He could kill
me.

"I thought you didn't remember writing it," said Mac,
smiling at the approaching town.

SOMEBODY HAD BOUGHT a newspaper and it lay splayed across one of the tables in the main hall. There was news from her city, and news from overseas—all the news she didn't want. She was thinking about throwing it away when Herb wandered in from the cafeteria, noticed Sara hovering, and asked if she was reading it.

"No," said Sara. "No one should be reading it."

"It's sad," said Herb, settling into a chair. "But we have to live in this world, don't we, retreat or no? We can't close our eyes to these things, much as we want to. That's what writers do. We face up."

Some of the participants heard what Herb was saying and inched closer. Sara had noticed this on several occasions—Herb wandering into the main hall with a cup of coffee, initiating a conversation, waxing casually profound on the subject of writing until he had gathered a tiny, devout clan around his chair.

"War," said Herb, scanning the front page. "Are you telling me you haven't considered writing something about the war—if you haven't written something already?"

"I refuse," said Sara, feeling the perverse adamancy descend again. She had written a handful of terrible poems only a few months ago.

Herb's talking about the war, someone called nearby.

"Oh, Sara, don't," said Herb, as if she were hurting him. "Don't refuse. Don't turn your back. If writers refuse to discuss these issues, where does that leave us?"

"You cheapen it," said Sara. "You cheapen it when you give it words. The more you talk about it, the more commonplace and mundane it becomes, until we're all going, *oh yeah, the war, war—war war war. It's just war.*" Sara felt itchy all of a sudden, wanting to scratch herself like a monkey. "We work in a pretty cheap medium, really."

Betty was walking past. She caught what Sara had said and laughed explosively.

"Let's all stop writing!" exclaimed Betty, not slowing down on her way to wherever she was going.

"Yes," said Sara, "let's stop." She turned around and saw Terry, who smiled and gestured to her.

I'm being called to the principal's office, thought Sara. But that wasn't something so much in her experience as it was the rest of the world's—the outside world's. To her it was just an expression—one of the many exotic, puzzling expressions she heard after leaving the family, like *pushing the envelope* and *don't be hatin'*. Growing up behind the mountains, Sara was only ever called into her father's office. Her father's office was wherever he happened to be.

She sat across from Terry, who had nice blue eyes and laugh lines and loved a good Gordon Lightfoot singalong. Plus, he was no more than six years older than her. Plus, she had done nothing wrong and was being ridiculous because she was sweating and closed-mouth panting the way she had done on the plane.

"How are things?" said Terry.

And it was also like her shrink's office, when the province decided she had to see a shrink before she could be declared an independent minor. *How are things*, that was how the meetings started. Sara's shrink had been a woman, however. One of the social workers had insisted on it— Sara found that out later, poring over her own files for the memoir. She had lied to Mac about that — she *had* conducted research on herself.

"Things are great, Terry."

"Week's gone okay?"

"It's been great, yeah. Wonderful group."

"Mm-hmm?" His eyebrows went up. "Any stars this year?"

There were no stars, but Sara threw out Alison's name to make Terry happy.

They smiled at each other, Sara relaxing a little. Maybe Terry was holding these impromptu, individual meetings with all the instructors.

"I wanted to ask you," said Terry, "if everything's okay in your bathroom."

Sara sat for a moment.

"With your toilet and everything," Terry prompted.

She burst into laughter like Betty.

"Oh my gosh! Yes! I'm sorry, Terry, I should have mentioned —"

Terry started to shake his head rapidly and wave his hands. "Yes, the maintenance guy had it fixed by the end of the day, no problem, no problem at all."

"Because," said Terry. "I was going to say, we could always switch your room, if you're having any problems."

Sara shook her head back at him. "Oh God, no, it's fine, it's been fine all week."

Terry didn't seem to be absorbing her reassurances. He pressed his lips together and inhaled through his nose.

"So the *shower* and everything is —"

"Shower, sink, toilet," recited Sara. "Everything's great."

Terry blinked his fine blue eyes at her.

"I mean," said Sara. She thought for a moment about the shower. "I can't quite remember if —" She tried to imagine the taps, the nozzle. Tried to conjure up a picture in her mind.

Suddenly her hands darted to her scalp. She looked down at her palms like they had come away bloody.

SHE'D BEEN TO these retreats before, both as a mentor and mentee—to use Terry's jargon—and there was always at least one person in attendance who was the person everybody talked about. Once it had been a young instructor who systematically slept with every female member of his group and then went on to infiltrate the others—it was like he had a checklist. Once it was a fiction student who refused to talk to any of the other participants and just sat staring at them with his eyes slitted like a cat's and his fingers forming a steeple when everyone came together for meetings or mealtimes. It got so no one was able to eat in his presence. Once it was a woman who was believed to be shrieking every night in her sleep, until someone reported that she wasn't sleeping at all—she was making these noises wide awake.

That is to say, there was always an odd person out at these things, always a weirdo.

She was clean for the reading with Marguerite, having sat under the shower for twenty shame-soaked minutes after talking to Terry. It hadn't turned on immediately. She was just thinking she would have to march her filthy-headed way back down the hall to his office when the nozzle hacked up a few squirts of tobacco brown, and finally silver jets began to spray out.

How could she have gone five days without taking a shower? She wondered if something had happened when she was up on the plane — if some fundamental part of her brain containing the instinct to bathe had been fried by the lightning jolt. The flight attendant told them the bolt had come out of nowhere — there'd been no indication of lightning anywhere in the sky before it hit. But what happens sometimes, he explained, is that the plane *causes* the lightning to occur. It flies through a charged cloud and the lightning actually originates from the plane.

"It came from *us*," said the flight attendant into his little intercom.

MARGUERITE GOT UP and read a poem about Marie. She was nowhere near the poet Betty was, and read like she was reciting from a grocery list. Plus, the poem was bleak. It was clear Marguerite wasn't kidding herself when it came to Marie's likely fate. There was a line about the winter fields screaming up at the sky that made Sara wince. One person noisily swallowed a sob and Terry stared at Marguerite, the fatherly cheer gone out of his eyes.

"Um," said Marguerite when she was finished. Behind her glasses she had a sweet, round face with a bow mouth like a fifties starlet. "I'm sorry if that was unexpected, I know poetry isn't my forte."

"It was *wonderful*," said Betty and started clapping. A

couple of people in Betty's group made noises of agreement and picked up the applause.

Marguerite looked around, gathered up her pages and
left the podium, which was awkward because she was
expected to read for another fifteen minutes or so.

Sara was in the middle of a glass of wine, so took it to
the podium with her after Terry's listless introduction. It
was up to her to salvage the mood, which was fine. Sara
was good at readings. She had a standard twenty minutes
of all the most compelling bits from her short story collection, tightly arranged and well rehearsed. She knew just
which phrases to punch, precisely how long to make her
pauses for maximum comedic effect. It was the same little
song and dance she'd been putting on for quite some time
in the hope of getting people more interested in her fiction.

She held up the book and was happy to disappear
behind it for a while. She was better at reading than she
was at talking—or even writing, she sometimes thought.
Everyone laughed at the spots where she knew they would
laugh, and clapped with apparent sincerity when she was
done. She shut her book and drained her wine, smiling.

"What about questions for Sara?" called Terry. Mac's
big hand poked up like a gopher's nervous head.

"I would really appreciate," said Mac, "a quick reading
from *Escaping Eden*."

"Yeah!" said Betty, clapping, clattering her bangles.

It was Marguerite's fault for finishing early—leaving
Sara all this extra time. "I don't have a copy with me,"
she protested. But Terry was already on his feet and at the
book table.

"It would mean a lot to me," said Mac.

She took the copy from Terry, opened it up to the first page and started plowing through the first paragraph. This, she remembered, was how she used to do readings when she was starting out. It never occurred to her to comb through the book, picking out the best-written sections. In Sara's opinion, there were no particularly well-written sections in *Escaping Eden*. People liked it because it was about teenage girls and sex and God and suffering. It was, in other words, a soap opera.

She read the words like they were someone else's—stumbling, missing key inflections, having to go back and start entire sentences again. The book started at the end of the story—a fairly conventional structure, suggested by her editor—with the night of Sara's escape. The rest of the chapters would fill in the background of her grotesque upbringing. When the book was released, she remembered, no one could believe such a community still existed. People were appalled—that is, they purported to be appalled, even though Sara remembered how gawkers from Creston and other nearby places used to cruise the village daily wearing faces of delight. She had said this in interviews.

Back then, she told everybody everything—every shameful detail. She couldn't have shut up if she tried. And people believed her, they heard her, they were every bit as angry as she was. She was soaring on outrage, the energy of having it released, as if she'd been flung from a slingshot.

She remembered the feeling of swooping across the country like a giant, avenging eagle. It was a dumb, obvious image, but that's how she remembered feeling—she'd grown up watching eagles, making mini gods of them. She didn't know enough back then to reject them as hackneyed. She wrote about eagles in the diary that became her book—their lizard eyes and pitiless heads. But her editor told Sara to take the eagles out. It was overused, amateurish symbolism, the editor said.

Sara hadn't read this bit in well over a decade, and found herself becoming fascinated, despite her clumsy reading, by what was happening in the pages—how the girl just climbed out of bed one night and left under cover of darkness. Where, Sara wondered, did that girl find the strength? She'd been told all her life she didn't have any— why didn't she believe it? She moved through the night without a doubt in her mind, jumped into one stranger's car and then the next. How did she get so sure of herself? Why wasn't she afraid? How could she be so certain she was right and they were wrong?

Afterwards, Betty unveiled a bottle of gin and bag of limes. Everyone had one more workshop left, but it wouldn't be until tomorrow afternoon and they were all too psychically exhausted to prepare. They acknowledged this to each other before starting to drink. The final workshop, everyone agreed once Terry was out of earshot, would be a hungover formality.

"I never imagined this would be such a wringer," said Alison, who looked like she might start crying for about the seventh time that week. "I thought—you know—it will be a nice little break, I'll learn some tricks. I wrangled PD money out of my company and everything—they're going to want to see *results*." Alison laughed like Betty—a desperate bray. "I can't very well come back and tell them, well, my copy hasn't really improved, but I spent ten days, you know, marinating in despair."

"*Marinating*," someone murmured. "That's good, I like that."

"Thanks for doing that," Mac said to Sara at one point, looking ashamed of himself.

Marguerite was sitting drinking red wine beside a couple of poets who were engrossed in conversation with each other. Sara came and sat beside her.

"Ah!" she said as a way of announcing herself.

Marguerite looked up, glasses like a shield. "I enjoyed your reading very much," she recited.

"Yours too," said Sara.

"I think it was a mistake," said Marguerite.

"Oh, it's all a mistake," said Sara, waving a hand. She was flying on the dregs of her pre-reading adrenalin.

"I'm just tired of the weirdness around it," said Marguerite. "All those posters, the fixation. I just want people to let her go, to quit messing with her."

"*Like a balloon pushing at the sky*," said Sara, surprising herself. She had produced a quote from Marguerite's poem.

"Ugh," said Marguerite. "I'm just not a poet. But what do you do when you're not a poet?"

"No, it's a good image," said Sara. "It's a simple, childhood image."

Marguerite's bow mouth puckered slightly. "*Surrender Dorothy*," she said. "We need something like that, some announcement. Written in the sky so everyone can see it. Surrender Marie, everybody. Give her up. It's time."

Sara folded her arms like her brother would have done and grunted as if from beneath a moustache: "It's about time they started bombing *something*." Blushing as Marguerite, in her confusion, looked down and then away.

ONCE, SHE USED to put herself to sleep like this:

There is no family. There is no Eden. There are no mountains. There is no Heaven. There is no Earth. There are no people. There are no places. There are no *names*.

It was the *names* line that worked best, that brought her to the next level, caused her body to feel as if it had gently pulled itself into fragments, which now were drifting in opposite directions. The next level went:

There is space. There is only space. Black, empty, infinite, all. There is I. I am space. Black and empty. I am all. Stretching, infinite, everything. I am everything. I am all. I am space.

SHE WOKE IN that darkness with a boom and a flash. People screamed and cursed convulsively, craned their bodies toward the windows. A distant alarm went off, low but insistent. Sweat blossomed from her pores, blotting against her clothes. There was laughter. It was still dark. Sara fell out of bed. Smoke filled the cabin. No it didn't. It seemed to—the seats and heads and stewardesses before her eyes went fuzzy. She couldn't smell the smoke. She bashed her hand against the corner of her desk. Something fell off the wall that had to be a picture of Christ, because that was the only thing they had on the walls. This is the nightmare, said Sara to herself. This is the thing that people say is like a nightmare.

There was a boom and a flash as she jerked open the door. One Easter, as a child, she woke in terrified, ecstatic tears after dreaming of the crucifixion all night long. She was Simon Peter and Jesus had flung himself into her arms. He was afraid; he didn't want to go. The social worker hadn't been able to hide her disgust. The EXIT signs glowed red. Sara moved through the red dark, trying to remember which room it was, the hallway crammed with smoke and panicked voices. She went from one door to the next, grasping and then releasing doorknobs, moving down the hall, in search of him.

THE NATURAL ELEMENTS

THE NATURAL ELEMENTS

Cal's daughter was always telling him what he could and couldn't say. She kept reminding him that he was retired—unlike every single one of her friends' fathers—therefore unacceptably old, therefore doddering around in a kind of anachronistic limbo that was deeply mortifying for those forced to live in close proximity to him. One thing he wasn't allowed to do, she'd informed him, was to say that his tenant had a silly name. Rain was his name.

"How is that spelled?" Cal asked, when he met with Rain's wife to have her sign the lease. He couldn't remember the wife's name because he'd been so bowled over, when they met, by the fact that her husband's name was Rain.

"Rain," said the wife. "R-A-I-N."

"Like rain from the sky," said Cal.

"Yes," agreed the wife.

Cal thought she looked a bit embarrassed.

Cal had never met Rain. In July the couple moved into the tiny post war house he owned (bought in 1989 for $30,000 and now with a market value, everyone kept shrieking at him, of at least $300,000). Rain had just been hired by the political science department at the university, and was never home. Cal only ever dealt with the wife.

"She's a stay-at-home wife?" demanded his daughter, Terry.

"Yes," said Cal. This new term: stay-at-home wife. How was it different from *housewife?* Who had found it necessary to make the change? This was something else he was not allowed to say.

"But she must do some kind of work," insisted Terry.

"Well, I don't know," said Cal. "Maybe she's looking."

He stood up from the table to find the HP Sauce and paused to pet his daughter's head a couple of times. He didn't know how else to show affection anymore. Anyway, it was instinctive with him. Her hair was so straight and smooth; it invited hands. Sometimes, petting her head, he would sigh dreamily, "I wish we had a dog," and leap out of reach as Terry whirled to punch him. Soon she would move away from home. She wanted to go to an elite arts college in Montana to study dance. The only reason he'd held on to the house near the university for so long was so that she could live in it while she attended school in the city.

"Whatareya gonna do with the house?" everybody slobbered at him. Big money! Big payoff! To own property that close to the university was, this past year, like sitting in your backyard and having the ground suddenly start to rumble and spew oil like on *The Beverly Hillbillies*. It was a city of Beverly Hillbillies lately — everyone cashing in. But Terry still could change her mind. Surely someone out there—not him, but someone at school, some adult she actually looked up to, her band teacher maybe—would talk her out of studying dance. He'd made the mistake of calling it *dancing* once, in front of some relatives who'd been passing through town. "Terry thinks she'd like to study dancing." The *thinks* had been bad enough. Calling it *dancing*, however, he still hadn't lived down.

Cal had a knack for tenants. As a rule, he didn't rent to undergraduates. Not that he had the instinctive loathing and distrust of them that some of his property-owning neighbours did, but just because he knew that if he wanted to keep the place in decent shape for Terry, he couldn't have kids in their early twenties living there. He rented to graduate students—most often couples—or sessional instructors, or new professors like Rain. People in training for home ownership and the middle class. Good tenants appreciated reasonable rent at a time when everyone living near the university was being milked like cattle, so when they moved out they recommended equally good tenants, who would appreciate it in turn. If you treated people fairly, they returned the favour. You didn't just gouge people because you could—because it happened to be the thing to do.

Cal would never forget his first landlord. He'd gone up north on a construction job and rented a basement from one of the managers. The manager had stipulated no smoking and no drinking.

"Fine," said Cal.

"No visitors," added the manager about a month after Cal had moved in.

"Pardon?" said Cal.

"No visitors."

"Oh, okay," said Cal, who didn't know anybody anyway.

"No music," added the landlord shortly thereafter.

"I'm sorry," said Cal. "Was I playing the radio too loud? I can turn it down."

"No," said the landlord. "You don't turn it down. You turn it off."

Three months into the rental, Cal realized he was brooding about the landlord almost every waking moment. Whispering outraged comments to himself on his way down the hill to the site, gritting his teeth over the circular saw, breaking into a frustrated sweat at the thought of going home in the evenings.

I hate going *home*, he kept thinking to himself. He has made it so I can't stand to go home.

So Cal started staying out.

"No staying out past ten," the landlord said to him one morning when Cal was on his way down the walk.

Cal stopped and turned around. The landlord was standing by his Honda, key in hand. He had offered to drive Cal to work every morning, but Cal had made excuses about enjoying the walk—the site was just down the hill. It was what had made the rental so attractive in the first place.

Cal walked over and stood on the other side of the landlord's Honda as if he had changed his mind about the drive and was about to climb into the passenger's side.

"Pardon?" he said.

"No staying out past ten," repeated the landlord. "We can't have you waking us up at all hours."

"That's ridiculous," said Cal.

"Well, that's the rule, I'm afraid."

"You can't treat people like this," said Cal. His armpits blasted sudden heat.

The landlord looked astonished. "I *own* this property," he told Cal, gesturing at the house behind him. "This is my property."

The way he made these statements—as if they were even pertinent, as if they answered for everything—stayed with Cal for years. When Cal built his own home—and then, on a whim, purchased the house near the university—he made a vow to himself with his first landlord in mind.

"I'm here to pull some snow off the roof," he said to Rain's wife.

"You're here to . . . ?" she repeated, looking worried.

I should have called first, thought Cal. "I'm sorry," he said, "I should have called. It's just that it's not good for all that snow to be piled up there."

"Oh!" said Rain's wife. Now she looked guilty.

"It's my job to look after this sort of thing," Cal assured her. It wasn't really. But Rain and his wife, Cal knew, were from somewhere unspeakably cruel, considering the deep-freeze they had moved to. Santa Cruz, California. Terry had been excited by this. It was the reason she wouldn't leave him alone about the tenants. That magic word: California.

So Rain and his wife couldn't be expected to under-stand the culture of cold and all it required. Moments ago when he approached the house, for example, he'd almost dislocated a hip slipping on a frozen sediment of snow that had caked up on the second step. They hadn't shovelled, and there had been some melt, and the snow had solidified into ice.

"Maybe I'll just clear your steps for you while I'm here," said Cal.

"Oh," said Rain's wife a second time. "You don't have to do that."

"Well," said Cal, and stopped himself from finishing: *somebody does.* "You could hurt yourself."

Cal asked her about the salt and the chipper in the basement, and once it was clear she had no idea what he was talking about, he asked if he could retrieve them himself. She backed into the foyer, saying, "Of course, of course." Californians, thought Cal, bending over to pull off his Sorels. You'd think Californians would be — I don't know. More sure of themselves. Rain's wife seemed so timid and deferential. Terry would be disappointed, to say the least. He took off his boots in the foyer and saw there was no mat nearby. Salt and grit from previous outings had discoloured the hardwood floor.

"Cal," said Rain's wife. "Now that you're here, could you do me a favour? Could you check out the furnace?"

Cal stood there noticing two things simultaneously. The floor was cold. It was so cold, the chill was already seeping through his thermal socks. And Rain's wife was wearing a fleece jacket over a thick wool sweater. As Cal registered this, she wiped her nose — twitchy and pink, like a rat's — on the sleeve of it.

He picked up his boots and carried them with him to the basement.

It was only when he returned to deliver the space heater that she told him Rain had gone. He was leaning over, after plugging the thing in, holding his hand in front of it to make sure it worked. She leaned over to do the same. They stood there, leaning together, feeling for heat.

"There it is," said Cal after a moment. He wiggled his fingers. "It doesn't feel like much right now, but these things are great. We used to use them on construction sites."

"It's just," said Rain's wife, "that Rain is gone."

Cal straightened up a bit creakily. His hands went to the small of his back. Rain's wife was rubbing her nose on her sleeve again.

"He's not here?"

"You're —" said Rain's wife. "I've been meaning to tell you. I mean, you're the landlord. It's just me living here now."

"Oh, I see," said Cal.

He drove home troubled.

"About how old is she, Dad?" Terry wanted to know.

Cal guessed about thirty-five, unaware of the trap he'd just stepped into.

"Thirty-five, Dad? A thirty-five-year-old *girl*?"

Cal rolled his eyes. He mentioned that Rain's wife had struck him as "a nice girl." This was something else he couldn't say.

"Well, what's she going to do?" asked his wife, Lana, as Terry guffawed over her spaghetti. "Is she moving out?"

"She didn't say," said Cal. "She just said she's by herself now."

"What happened to the husband?"

"I don't — Terry, will you stop?" Terry was making a big production of pounding her fist on the table, convulsed with mirth. She was at the age where she took everything too far. Actually, it seemed to Cal that she should have passed through this phase long ago.

It snowed again and didn't stop for three days. He thought of her, alone in the house. He picked up his address book and dialled the number he'd scrawled beneath the word *Rain*.

"Hello there," he said when she picked up. He was calling her "there" because he didn't know her name. "It's Cal. How are you getting along in all the snow?"

"Oh," she said, "I keep thinking I should shovel, but there doesn't seem to be any point!"

You should shovel anyway, thought Cal. The neighbours. And she seemed to have no idea it was also her responsibility to clear the sidewalk in front of the house. But he said, "No, I know. It's, ah — it seems like an, an exercise in futility."

"That's exactly it," she said. "It's like an insult."

"Insult to injury," replied Cal.

"Yes," she answered faintly.

Cal pictured her rubbing her twitchy rodent's nose on the sleeve of her fleece, saying, It's just me now.

"Not like California!" he crowed, suddenly hearty.

She laughed like a sob down the wire.

Terry, home from school because of the snow and still in pajamas at two in the afternoon, stood in the living room window watching him plow the walk on his ride-on.

Then he trundled down the sidewalk, clearing that, and finally cleared the walks of the neighbours on either side. It took no time at all and was an easy enough courtesy.

"You looked so happy," Terry told him when he came in. "You looked like you would've cleared every driveway on the block if you could get away with it. That's so sad, Dad. You are such a sad, sad man." She flounced away with her hot chocolate.

When the snow stopped, he loaded his plow into the back of the truck, drove north toward the university and thanked God for four-wheel drive when he turned onto the apocalyptic side streets. City hall was being bombarded with complaints, because it contracted snow removal out to private companies, and the private companies answered to no one. They were too busy, they claimed. There was the Costco parking lot to be cleared, the Best Buy. Cal bounced over Himalayas of ice and packed drifts. Past buried cars. It was like with construction these days — too much work, too few companies. There were always bigger, more lucrative jobs. Workmen tore holes in people's walls, went away, and never returned.

What was the good of all this money? If it made no one responsible to anyone else? If it made life not easier, but in some cases impossible? He thought this as he pulled up to the non-existent sidewalk of Rain's wife's house; buried, like everything, in snow. There she stood, up to her knee-caps in it, stabbing wildly at the second step with the ice chipper. It made an awful, echoing clang every time it hit concrete. When it didn't hit concrete, when it just bounced uselessly off the unyielding ice, it made an unsatisfying *thuck*. The sound of her helplessness dully resonating. Another insult.

The furnace man had not come. Cal was incredulous.

"You're kidding."

"They're probably so busy this time of year."

"Yes but—Jesus Christ," said Cal. "I called three weeks ago."

"The space heater works fine," she assured him.

Cal frowned at it. She was responsible for the electricity bill. It would be through the roof by month's end.

"Listen, dear," he said. Terry would castrate him for calling a grown woman "dear," but he had to call her something. "Take a hundred dollars off the rent this month."

She blinked at him. She was wearing the same fleece over a thick turtleneck. Over the fleece she had draped the knitted throw that, during his last visit, had adorned her shabby ottoman. The ottoman, he noticed, was nowhere in sight. The place was only semi-furnished now. Rain had subtracted his things, presumably, and the room stood half nude, throwing weird echoes now that there was less furniture to absorb human voices.

"Cal," she said, softly, because she wasn't so stupid as to dig in her heels about the rent. "There's no —"

"No, no," he shouted, causing her to cringe a little. He just wanted the conversation with its hollow echoes to end. "It's absurd. It's just absurd," he said. And went outside to finish de-icing her step, forgetting to say goodbye. Then he changed the blade on his snowplow and annihilated the layers of tramped-down snow that had caked up where the sidewalk used to be.

He sat in his truck and took out his phone in order to yell at the furnace man—a man he knew, a man named Mike—but all he got was a recorded, vaguely seductive female voice, which informed him Mike's inbox was full.

He looked up at the house and Rain's wife was staring out her window at him, just standing there, not looking off or turning away as he gazed back, as if she wasn't aware she was doing it.

"Why don't you go home?" he said out loud.

The wife was a web consultant, she'd mentioned back in July. What did that mean? Terry had told him that anything having to do with the internet meant pornography. The only people who made any money via the internet, she said, were pornographers. They were legitimate business people now, she proclaimed, not sleazy pervert types. They had BlackBerrys and took meetings and it was good business, just like anything, just like oil and gas. Some of them were even women. (Oh good, thought Cal. Terry is considering this. This is her fallback if dancing doesn't work out.)

So Cal could only assume that Rain's wife made no money. He imagined her work as a "web consultant" to be one of those nominal jobs that stay-at-home wives sometimes had. A job that wasn't actually meant to furnish any income other than what his mother used to call "pin money." That was why she didn't go back to California. Rain's wife was trapped.

"Terry is too confident," Cal told Lana one night.

Lana laughed at him.

"I don't think you understand," he persisted. He wasn't

sure how to approach this with her. It required laying out the kind of home truths women seldom liked to hear.

"Confidence is good, Cal. We want our daughter confident."

Lana had stopped speaking to her own father at the age of twenty-five. She didn't know he had died until a couple of weeks afterward, because her mother had long since passed, and her other sister didn't speak to him either. And when she did find out, Lana gave no indication that she cared. Lana's father had terrorized and oppressed both daughters every day of their lives. They couldn't date, they couldn't go out, they had to come home immediately after school, they would not be sent to college because college was the place where women behaved like sluts.

"We will not be doing that to our daughter," Lana told Cal, often.

So Cal had been terrorized in turn with the idea that if he ever spoke a word of reproach to any of the females of his household, their mouths would snap shut and they would saunter out from under his roof, leaving him to age in silence, to decompose in an empty house.

"She takes certain things for granted," Cal persisted.

"Like what?"

"Like her safety. She's sheltered, she's protected. She's lived a comfortable life, and she thinks she's invulnerable."

"Well, let her think it."

"No," said Cal. "She'll be going to Montana, or wherever, next year. She knows nothing about it. The world is a dangerous place. What about all those street women who were murdered?"

"What we do is," smirked Lana, "we take precautions. We discourage the use of crystal meth, for example. I think we should take a hard line on that."

At that point, Cal climbed out of bed and put on his bathrobe all in one motion.

"Cal," said Lana, startled.

"I'm not a fool," said Cal.

His daughter wrestling with him when she was little, angry that he could so effortlessly break out of her grip. She wanted him to pretend that she was stronger than he was, and he of course had obliged, bemused but also a little horrified. The blithe way women took the gentleness of men for granted. The kindness of strangers. Early in his marriage to Lana, he'd been stunned to realize how different their perception of sex was. While he was ever aware of how protective, how careful he was being with her, it seemed she never was. This amazed and troubled him, because for Cal, the restraint was part of the sweetness. He could have been rough with her, could have grabbed her and pushed her and maybe she would have even liked it, but he never did. It didn't seem to occur to Lana that things could be any other way. This was the stunner: she didn't even know. My dear, he wanted to say to his daughter sometimes, if a two-hundred-pound man wants to drag you into an alley, he will drag you into an alley. It won't matter how well you do in school or how assertive you are with telemarketers. It won't matter how many times you correct an old man for calling a woman a "girl." You're still going into that alley. It is an ugly thing to think, and to say, but there you go.

"MIKE," CAL SAID to the furnace man. "Five weeks now, Mike."

"You have no idea of our workload right now, Cal."

"This is *north*," said Cal. "It's *February*. People could freeze to death. Senior citizens living by themselves..."

"No one's freezing to death, Cal," said Mike. "My God. Just get her a space heater, you're the landlord."

"You are...an asshole, Mike," Cal stuttered.

He'd never said this to another man before, and he'd never hung up on anyone. It enraged him that he didn't know how to fix a furnace in his own house. If he proposed to have people living under his roof, wasn't it incumbent upon him to ensure that the necessities of life, such as warmth in the wintertime, were provided? Money wasn't enough. That was the mistake men always made — assuming money was enough. To think that he could end up the kind of man who was helpless without money, who wasn't able to just do it himself if he couldn't pay someone else to do it, made him sick. Because that wasn't a man. That was just another kind of asshole.

It went to forty below.

When he arrived, she was outside, flailing away at the sidewalk. She wore her hood up and a toque pulled down over her eyebrows, and a voluminous cotton scarf wrapped around everything but her eyes. She looked like one of those veiled women from the Middle East, except puffed out by her down coat, and with a gargantuan head. Nothing visible but squinting eyes. Crisp white clouds plumed from beneath the scarf and hung in the air like solid objects.

"I *love* this," she said to Cal as he approached. She had figured out how to use the chipper. She lodged it beneath a layer of ice and then threw her weight upon it and an enormous wedge of the ice layer broke off and came free of the sidewalk.

Cal understood her satisfaction immediately—force overcoming resistance, over and over again. He surveyed her work. She'd cleared the entire walk and had done about a foot of sidewalk. But it was a big lot. There were hours of work ahead of her, which he doubted she would finish by sunset.

"That must've taken you all day," he said.

"It did," she said. "I thought I would hate it, but I love it. It's therapeutic."

"But, dear," he said. "This temperature—you're making it too hard on yourself. Better to wait until it warms up a bit."

"I can't," she told him. "I got a note from the city this morning."

This broke Cal's heart and enraged him all at once. The city—the city who would not even clear the street—had left a note in the mailbox of his house, demanding he live up to his most basic responsibilities as a homeowner.

"And the mailman left a note too," she added. "He stopped delivering the mail."

Mail-person. Letter carrier. Postal worker. She had no idea what she was doing to Cal.

"I'm so sorry," he fretted. "About the furnace. I just don't know when the guy'll be out."

"Oh—" She pulled down her cotton scarf a little to wipe the condensation off her face, and he could almost feel the moisture freezing his own cheeks. "The space heater's fine. And I started cooking roasts! I never cooked roasts before. I used to be a vegetarian."

Cal could only stare at her.

"It heats up the kitchen," she explained. "Cooking roasts."

He had an image of her huddled in front of the space heater amongst her bare-bones furniture, gnawing away at a glistening slab of pork butt. Instead of dropping to his knees before her on the patch of sidewalk she'd managed to unearth, he turned and made for his truck.

"Call me," he yelled without turning his head. "Just call me if you need anything."

He did not phone to check up on her for well over a month. He had never avoided anyone out of shame before.

Then spring happened, the way it sometimes does in extreme climates. That is, it broke wildly over the city like a piñata. Sun and heat blazed down and suddenly there were rivers of melt in the streets. A new kind of chaos took over as the city overflowed. Cal knew his own basement would be fine, because he had built it himself. But he wondered about hers. He hadn't been to her basement since he went down to get the salt and chipper—months ago. He tried to remember if she had anything important-looking stored down there. If she's having any trouble, he told himself, she'll call. And she didn't.

Terry would graduate in a few months. They still hadn't heard back from Montana, but he had persuaded her to apply to the local university as a fail-safe, and she'd been accepted.

"Whatever," Terry had said, refolding the acceptance letter.

"Whatever," repeated Cal. "I'm getting one of the best educations in the country. I get an entire house to live in for free—whatever. Tuition has gone up another twenty percent and my education is bought and paid for. Whatever."

Lana, who had been putting away groceries with her usual impatient rush, glanced over and started moving in slow motion as if he'd pulled a gun.

"All right, Dad," said Terry, rising so as not to be in the same room with him anymore.

Rents in the city had skyrocketed in the past year. A basement "studio" for twelve hundred dollars. He'd read a piece in the paper that said five Chinese exchange students had been discovered living practically stacked on top of one another in such a place. Fire hazard, said the city. The landlord denied any wrongdoing and was contesting it. These people gotta live somewhere, he told the reporters.

Cal started fantasizing about calling Rain's wife in June and telling her she had to move out by the summer because Terry needed to move in for school. It started out as a kind of masochism, taking root in his guilt and dread. But he kept coming back to the scenario, rehearsing it a little too compulsively, and after a while it became almost pleasurable to contemplate. He imagined her helpless, flailing silence.

But Cal, she would stammer at last. I don't have any money.

Not my problem, I'm afraid.

I don't know anybody here. Wherever shall I go? Whatever shall I do?

Frankly, my dear...

Please, Cal. I'm begging you.

I'm sorry, Rain's wife. (No, he wouldn't even say he was sorry. He didn't have to say that.) I can't help you, Rain's wife. There's nothing I can do for you. Absolutely nothing. You have one month. To get out. To get the hell out. To hell with you.

Then, as if she had heard all this — as if the shameful echoes in his head had somehow transmitted themselves to her — she called.

"It's Angie," she said.

"What?" said Cal, even though he'd recognized her voice at once.

"Angie. At the house?"

"Oh, yes. Hi, Angie," said Cal.

"How are you?" she said.

"I'm fine, dear," said Cal. "Everything okay?"

"All of a sudden," she said, laughing a little, "it's so warm!"

"I know," he said. "Strange weather."

"I see there's an air conditioner in the basement."

It was too early for an air conditioner. And not nearly hot enough to justify one. She was supposed to be from California.

"Oh dear," he said. "You have to understand about the weather here. We're just as likely to get another snowstorm next month."

She laughed again like he was kidding. "I was going to

fire it up," she said. "But then I realized the storm windows were still up."

"Honestly, dear," he said, "I'd keep them up for a while yet." And how did she suppose she was going to get the air conditioner up the stairs herself?

"It's just so warm," she persisted. "And I can't really open the windows to get a cross breeze."

"Right," he said. "Well, I could come by."

"Would you?"

"Of course," he said.

But he put it off for over a week. Then she called again.

Cal apologized. He'd been very busy. His daughter's graduation coming up. Lots of activity. To his surprise, the fine weather hadn't abated. He had supposed the temperature would drop again and she would see the wisdom of putting off the storm windows for later in the season. He told her he would stop by as soon as he had a moment. She was grateful. But he didn't go until the following Wednesday, and he didn't call to tell her he was coming.

"Oh no," he yelped at the sight of them. "No, no, no!"

Angie and a man were in the yard, struggling to remove one of the storm windows from its hooks at the top of the frame. It had come free of one hook, but they were having trouble with the other, so the entire five-by-three-foot pane was dangling by one corner. The man had barely the arm-span to manage it. They had dragged the picnic table, of all things, over to the side of the house and the man was standing on it, on his tiptoes, stretching to his very last inch in the attempt to hoist the window free of the hook. He didn't have the height or the strength for this. His T-shirt rode up and Cal registered a queasy contrast of black hair against white belly, the hair thickening considerably as it approached his crotch. This could only be Rain.

Angie stood on the ground beside him, ineffectually reaching up to steady the window.

It seemed only Cal was aware that the moment the thing came free of the hook, it would fall backwards, shattering on top of both their heads. Rain, face blank with exertion, glanced over as Cal scrambled up onto the table to take charge.

"Let's get it back up there," said Cal, grabbing a side. "Get it back on the other hook so you can take a rest."

Rain grunted in agreement and the two of them managed to reattach the other corner.

"This is Cal," Angie said from somewhere behind him.

Standing together on the brutalized, corpse-yellow lawn, the men shook hands.

"Rain," said Rain. He was wearing a sports jacket and black basketball sneakers. His T-shirt said *Talk Nerdy to Me*. His bushy head of hair, unlike the hair on his belly, was almost completely grey.

This was a professor, Cal reminded himself. At the university. The university had hired him to teach students political science. Would Terry be taking political science? Rain tried not to pant, his grey mop soaked in sweat. Cal wondered how long the two of them had struggled with the window. The thought of them like that—Rain helpless with the oversized pane, Angie helpless on the ground beside him, both about to be grated like cheddar—made his bowels flutter.

"Rain," repeated Cal, and the name was like a mouthful of spoiled food. "Listen, that window might be rusted onto the hook up there. You just leave it to me. I'll get a stepladder and —" at this point, had he been talking to Angie, Cal would have stopped himself— "do it properly."

"Yeah," agreed Rain. "Thanks, bro. Seriously. Angie says you've been great."

"Oh," said Cal, flustered by a near irresistible urge to shove Rain as hard as he was physically capable of doing.

"So I should get going," said Rain.

"I'd like a word with you," said Cal.

Angie went inside the house and the two of them stood in the alleyway together. Cal had no idea what he would say, he only knew he wanted to talk at this man. He felt it like a sudden, stabbing hunger, when you know you'll eat whatever's put in front of you. He opened his mouth and listened to himself as he would an authoritative voice on the radio.

"You have abandoned this girl," Cal heard himself saying. "This is Abandonment." He said it over and over again, hearing the capital A in his voice, as if he were charging Rain with a crime—wanting to impress upon him the seriousness of his transgression. Rain stood with his hands on his hips, gazing at the ground and shaking his head. Sometimes he shook it tightly, as if in defiance, and other times loosely, in apparent disbelief. Cal realized with disgust that Rain was never going to raise his head and look him in the eye.

At the same time, Cal knew men left women and women left men and it was all perfectly legal—even natural. It was a tragedy, but only in the way that all of nature was a tragedy. But there were rules, there were truths and virtues, and that was all he wanted Rain to acknowledge.

The question was, what if Rain didn't know? This is what kept Cal talking, fast and mindless, in a voice that sounded abraded and high-pitched, like Angie's chipper scraping concrete. What if Rain, who continued to stand there and shake his head with loose, angry amusement, who was from Santa Cruz, who merely wanted someone to talk nerdy to him—what if Rain had no idea what Cal was talking about? What if Rain was oblivious? What if Rain—who should have been laughable, and who instead made no one laugh—what if Rain, himself, laughed?

BODY CONDOM

BODY CONDOM

It had only been a handful of months since she agreed to
be in love with Hart. And now that she was, he kept issu-
ing edicts, startling her with statements like, "Seeing as it's
official now, we should probably cut out flirting. We need
to separate our flirting friends from our friend-friends."

She'd tell him, "I don't have flirting friends."

"Oh, sure you do."

"*You* have flirting friends. That's *all* you have. I barely
have friend-friends."

"Oh, I do not. You do so."

At first, deciding to be in love felt to Kim like a process
of having to explain to Hart, in different ways, every day,
that she was nothing like him. And Hart not believing her,
and her having to convince him. Then one day the process
came to an end—Hart abruptly agreed to consider each of
them as individual people with separate experiences and
differing points of view.

"You're not as gregarious as I am," Hart announced one

day after failing to drag her to a friend's open mic event. "You don't need as much social stimulation."

"That's right!"

"But I need a lot. I need a lot more than most people."

"It's true, Hart. You do."

"So I can just go out for a few hours, say hi to everybody. And you can just stay here," Hart hypothesized, frowning like he was trying to do math in his head. "And then I'll come back!"

Kim bobbed her head at him—encouraging.

"It'll be all right," Hart assured himself, fingering the jacket he always hung on the doorknob when he arrived.

"Now THAT WE'RE in love we need to have serious conversations. Okay? We really need to talk about real stuff. It can't just be superficial banter."

This was new. This was Hart, heralding an official New Stage.

"What?"

"We haven't really delved."

"I delve."

"No—we've been coasting. And it's been great—so great. Sexy repartee. Very Nick and Nora. But we have to get serious now."

"I'm always serious!"

"Don't get angry, honey. Things are changing, that's all. We're evolving as a couple."

And he had started to call her honey.

What was daunting for Kim, and what she was finding

difficult to express now that they were supposed to only talk seriously to one another, was that the whole reason she had agreed to be in love had to do with how Hart had behaved previous to the agreement. The way they had been together, at first. It was true that she had not taken Hart seriously for a very long time. "You weren't supposed to," Hart told her later. "That's my M.O." Hart was, by her reading, a walking erection. "I know!" agreed Hart. "I totally am. Was! Tee hee." She would see him at one of the cabaret nights, always insisting on going on first, it seemed to Kim, precisely so he could reap the maximum rewards of his onstage charm via several fulsome hours of female appreciation. As she prepared for her set, Kim would notice him slipping like mercury through the crowd, breastbone-first, a head taller than everyone else. Erect was the only word that fit. At practically every second woman Hart would exclaim in decibels that could be heard even above the sound system and dart forward for a hug—not so much a hug as what Kim came to refer to in her mind as The Great Enfolding.

After a few nights on the same bill, Kim inevitably became one of the enfolded. She didn't mind. She'd done her time with charismatic men, knew enough to enjoy the lingering hug for the warm, physical moment it was, never letting herself settle in too deep. But who was she to turn away a comforting expanse of male chest in the thick of an indifferent crowd?

"You have to teach me to play ukulele like you do!"

She laughed. Hart was a virtuoso. His set alternated between guitar, banjo and violin.

"It's four strings, Hart. I think you can figure it out."

"It's the way you play it, baby. Like you're nursing it. Like you're cradling a man's head."

"Okay, see you, Hart."

"That wasn't a reference to your breasts, exactly. It kind of was but—HOLY SHIT CONNIE! CONNIE IS THAT YOU? WHERE HAVE YOU BEEN ALL SUMMER, GIRL, GET *OVER* HERE!"

After a few months of more or less identical conversations—ecstatic greeting, Great Enfolding, compliment, innuendo, see you, Hart—she decided one night to change the script. It had been a grim set. Kim had recently decided to go all-ukulele and was discovering how the instrument antagonized a certain demographic. That night, the crowd was especially hostile due to a local Tom Waits wannabe on the bill who wrote songs about accidentally killing hookers during heroin binges in blood-spattered hotel rooms. Kim had it on pretty good authority this guy had grown up in West Point Grey, but his fans made up most of the crowd and some shit-faced bike courier with dried mud splattered across his leg tattoos kept shouting up at her: *Too old!*

So as Hart's friendly breastbone loomed closer, she did the obligatory leaning-in, submitted to the sweat-fragrant enfolding, made the requisite how-you-been small talk until the inevitable moment when she knew he would dangle his penis into the conversation like the proverbial worm on a hook. She told him, "I'm too old for this, Hart," slouching off toward the bathroom before he could recognize the next beloved woman of his acquaintance and wade, bellowing, in her direction.

Instead, Hart waded after Kim. "Me too!" he was calling. "I'm too old for this too!"

"THAT WAS THE moment," Hart said later. "That was the first real moment between us. When we cut through the bullshit. *You* did. We need more of those moments. It needs to be all those moments from here on in."

Kim was about to tell him she loved his superficial side as much as she loved anything else about him, his mesmerizing charm, his ease with the unnerving force of his own sexuality—the way he kept it at heel like it was nothing, like he was leading around a panther on a leash, but he'd grown up with the panther, the panther was no big deal to him, meanwhile people stood rigid and sweating as he passed.

She was about to tell him all that one afternoon as they sat in her apartment teaching themselves Gillian Welch, except Hart started to cry.

He'd been talking about *really* talking for the last month. It was only their second month of being officially in love. The first few months together had been sexual Disneyland—nothing but endorphins and giddy indulgence. It seemed early to be putting the brakes on that— this was Kim's guilty first thought.

She held his head against her like a ukulele and rocked.

HART DID NOT drink—that should have been her first hint. She had told herself this was refreshing. So many guys in her life did not know how to stop drinking like teenagers, because playing music kept you teenage in so many ways (in her twenties, that seemed like such an upside, and then in her thirties all of a sudden it didn't). Hart drank ginger ale and never remarked upon it, never told people he was "cutting back" or "had to stay sharp'" for his set—none of the excuses of social drinkers. This telegraphed a message to Kim that she ignored: *Note how cheerful and upbeat Hart is at all times. How hard at work.*

Hart drank only once, he told her, at fifteen, a few days after he ran away from home the first time, and disappeared for a month. He had taken his first sip of a friend's strawberry margarita at one end of Vancouver Island and woken up on the exact opposite end, on a bench overlooking Victoria harbour, almost five hundred kilometres south. There was a man in his sixties sitting beside Hart, a stranger in a yellow golf shirt with white blow-dried hair, his arm around him.

They were on the ferry to Port Hardy and the stories just kept coming. Hart drank one ginger ale after another as he talked. Sugar was his drug now. He told her it used to be cola, but he went crazy for the caffeine. "I have no impulse control," he told her. "Anything that affects my brain, I can't get enough of it." Not two years ago he was downing espressos on the hour. "I was in a state of crisis every minute of the day. Everything was so major! Everything felt crucial! I'd go to my friend's place and they'd say, Oh, we're out of milk and I'd be like OH MY GOD! WHAT IS TO BE DONE! And my heart was racing and life was just … so exciting! That was hard to walk back from. I was so depressed for like a year. Getting off caffeine is the hardest thing I've ever done, honey."

Everything he told her on that ferry ride was a blow to Kim; a shot to the kidneys. Because she understood their sex life now. She had thought they were so compatible. As her body crept toward forty—the way Hart had crept north along the highway, returning home on the Greyhound after his first and only blackout—her libido had gone from polite, to politely insistent, to beseeching, to basically a fire engine's siren. She started to understand the clichés of television—the embarrassing, oversexed Older Woman. She had split up with depressive Malcolm mid-beseeching phase, after eleven years together, five of them essentially sexless, and wanted nothing more than to sleep with anyone she had ever felt the remotest inkling toward. Six months of that kind of indulgence had been enough. There was no room for dignity in this new circumstance.

Things had been looking hopeless until Hart, man of boundless energy, boundlessly horny, declared himself to her. For a while, as he sprawled long-limbed around her apartment speaking of moving in together, a musical retreat on a lake somewhere in the interior, even making late-life babies, Kim had let herself imagine it might be possible to set up house in Disneyland on a permanent basis—to spend every day riding the rides, wind whipping your hair, fireworks nightly, gorging on nothing but hot dogs and cotton candy. Never getting sick, or full.

But it was just, she discovered on the ferry, that Hart was an addict; a sensation-junkie. He spoke to a counsellor every week, she learned, a woman he called "my lifeline."

And his mother was an addict, too, he told her. And his brother, who lived with his mother, was an addict, also clinically depressed. There had been "a couple of suicide attempts," confessed Hart, though he didn't bother to attach either attempt to anyone in his family specifically. It reminded Kim of her final few years with Malcolm, the monosyllables, the sleep-stink of the bedroom because the bed was never changed, because the bed never didn't have anyone in it, every day a sort of funeral—we are gathered here to say goodbye to our beloved childhood companion Fun; today we bury Careless Youth, taken from us too soon. It reminded her of the vow she'd made: *Never this again.*

They were on their way to see them—the brother and mother—and then Hart's rock-and-roll father, Wilf, who lived with his girlfriend farther down the coast. Kim and Hart sat on the deck, as close to the bow as they could, watching the ocean come at them, inhaling its molecules. She made herself imagine one vertebra of her spine after another turning into iron with every new family revelation of Hart's, until finally the metal would meet her brain stem and she would be nothing but fortitude.

But before that could happen, just before the ferry docked, he confessed to her the horror of his father and she stood up and walked to the other end of the ship. She didn't run. She told him she was going to buy chips. If she'd run Hart would've chased her.

IT WAS SUPPOSED to be a vacation. That's how he sold it to her. She would meet his family (it had sounded so innocent then, romantic, the next Big Step, another New Stage), but they would also have fun, because the island was beauti ful. They would camp on Long Beach and listen to waves the length of city blocks roll in. They would go surfing. There was a weekend yoga retreat run by a friend of his where they could "recharge after the family stuff," said Hart—so lightly, he had said this. Family stuff: childhood photo albums, stilted conversation, awkward getting-to-know-you back and forth on opposite sides of the kitchen table—that's what Kim had thought he meant by "family stuff." It had all been a plot. Hart had staged-managed the whole thing.

"We won't stay at my mother's," he assured her. The plan was to camp down the hill at the town's one campsite, called Ozzieland, after the owner, Ozzie. They checked in at Ozzieland before heading up to Hart's mother's house there was something unspoken and deliberate about this decision. They were the only campers, and Ozzie—a gnome-like senior citizen wearing the kind of glasses that used to be called old man glasses but now would be hip-ster, on someone like Hart, at least—was wildly happy to receive them. He hugged Hart, clearly as in love with him as everyone else, and invited them to dinner with himself and his wife that evening, or if not dinner then breakfast. Hart promised they'd stop in for coffee before hitting the road the next morning.

"Not a lot of visitors to Alice lately," Ozzie explained. That was what locals called the town, Port Alice. "Cuz of the mill, and the cougar. Not necessarily in that order."

"What about the mill?" said Hart, before Kim could ask about the cougar.

"Shut down."

"Shut down?" said Hart. "Holy shit."

"Holy shit is right," agreed Ozzie.

"It's the only thing in town," Hart explained to Kim.

"Mill town," affirmed Ozzie.

"How long?" asked Hart.

"What cougar?" said Kim.

"Just don't go for any walks," advised Ozzie. "Take your rental everywhere you go and you'll be fine. I mean she doesn't come into town, she stays pretty much on the outskirts so far, but then again she's getting bolder. You want to be careful."

So Kim and Hart got in their rental—a Nissan Cube, all that had been available from the Hertz in Port Hardy—and drove two minutes up the hill to meet Hart's people.

BRENDA'S HOUSE WAS mainly jungle. Hart's father had built it for her, for the two of them, twenty-five years ago. It was not the house Hart grew up in—Hart's hometown was Hardy. The bungalow in Alice was meant to be an oceanside retreat—a "love shack," Hart called it, smirking—so the entire front was sunroom, windows from ceiling to floor. Over the years, Brenda stuffed it full of plants, to the point where barely any sun filtered into the main room anymore—the plants made up a dappled, verdant wall and when the sun came level with the windows, as it was now, the living room shone green.

They sat in the green around the coffee table. Brenda had put out Chips Ahoy cookies on a plate and placed a two litre bottle of ginger ale beside it with two glasses full of ice. Then she went back to the kitchen, where she took a can of Blue Light from the fridge and poured it into a plastic tumbler for herself. She did not offer a Blue to Kim. Things were feeling stage-managed again, like the visit was unfolding according to certain guidelines.

"No caffeine, right, son?"

"Thanks for remembering, Brenda."

Kim had never met a mother who called her son "son" before. It got downright odd when her other son arrived. She called them both "son" then, and both sons called her Brenda, not Mom.

The two of them, Brenda and Arlo, were diminished versions of Hart. Smaller, paler. Hart minus yoga and running, minus energy and height.

Hart enfolded his brother as he had enfolded those countless women in bars, Arlo's face in Hart's chest. The brother tried to pull away after a moment and Hart said, "No, man." So they stood like that a little longer while Kim stared into the wall of the foliage. The effect was exactly like stained glass at church, if the glass was various hues of green.

"I love your plants, Brenda," she said as Arlo and Hart disengaged.

"Thanks, Kim." Brenda stood up and walked over to a grouping of geraniums. "These are my geraniums," she said.

My God, thought Kim, she's going to introduce me to her plants.

And that was just what Hart's mother did for the next twenty minutes, as Hart and Arlo murmured to one another at the far end of the couch.

THERE HAD BEEN no mention of Hart and Kim ditching Ozzieland and staying overnight at Brenda's, even after Kim had forced a long, exhaustive discussion of the cougar. Ozzie hadn't been lying when he said the cougar ("Or cougars," reflected Brenda) had not yet come into town. But she (the singular cougar was a she, apparently) had been spotted at either end, so the residents of Alice were effectively in prison. The town sat on a road along the ocean; behind them was woods. On either side of them was woods. The minute you hit the woods, you were in cougar territory. Which meant cougar on all sides.

Brenda drank one can after another of Blue Light and Hart kept pouring himself ginger ale as Kim nursed hers. Brenda eventually brought out the entire bag of Chips Ahoy! and handed it to Hart.

"Hart, stop," Kim muttered at one point, his hand in the bottom of the bag.

"How's Wilf?" Hart had asked about ten cookies in.

Brenda smiled and gestured with her plastic tumbler. "Oh—you know Wilf. Life of Riley down in Ucluelet."

"I see him sometimes," whispered Arlo as Kim clenched.

"Do you?" said Hart. "How's the old guy looking?"

"Hale and hearty," smiled Arlo. "You know Wilf."

MY GOD YOU PEOPLE, Kim wanted to yell.

"Same hair I bet," said Hart, grinning. "Like Samson. Never changes."

"Not our Wilf," said Brenda. "Ever the hippie."

The three of them laughed together anemically — their broken, family laughter. She had never heard Hart laugh that way before. Hart was the kind of person waiters in cafés had to ask to settle down. He was a head-thrower-backer.

"Kim and I are off to do yoga for a couple of days," said Hart, slinging an arm around her and popping the remaining Chips Ahoy! into his mouth.

SHE HATED HIM. She slept in the Cube. She didn't tell him it was because she was hating him, she said it was the cougar. It was, in fact, partly because of the cougar. But the cougar was a big part of the reason she was hating him.

Brenda had told her the cougar had killed one man, a hiker from the mainland. Dragged him off and his body had never been found. Another man, local fella, she had attacked recently, but did not succeed in killing. The man had a penknife on him, did battle with the cougar, and won — managed to saw at the animal's throat after gouging her eyes. This was impressive, but the unfortunate thing was that the cougar had initially got the jump on the man. Literally, she had jumped on him from behind, from an overhead rock. She had clawed his face off. The man was alive to tell the tale, but would never look the same. You might see him, Brenda told Kim brightly, like they were discussing a mutual friend. Walking around town.

Can't miss him, that's for sure. Keep your eye out tomorrow as you're leaving.

IT WAS AN eight-hour drive to Tofino, Hart announced. She couldn't believe it.

"But it's an island," she kept repeating.

"It's a big island. It's the biggest island on the entire west coast."

"It's gotta be the size of a country. Of Australia."

"It's actually pretty close to Taiwan."

"Well, this is ridiculous, Hart," said Kim.

Hart made an effort not to talk for a few minutes. He had that look on his face like he was trying to solve equations.

"Honey?" he said at last. "We have eight hours to hash this out. Then it's two days of yoga and camping and good food and I will not touch sugar and I guarantee you it's going to be gorgeous and beautiful and healing. Then — and only then — do we see Wilf. So let's hash this out."

A week ago she would've thought how much she loved being with a man who uttered words like *gorgeous* and *beautiful* and *healing* with total conviction, with no trace of masculine shame. Because beauty and healing were full-on good, in Hart's cosmology — not ironic, not ridiculous — and should be spoken of with reverence and sincerity. The men in Kim's family were nothing like Hart. To her knowledge, her brothers and father and uncles had never deemed any aspect of their world — not even a sunset, or a woman — gorgeous. Or if they had, they'd rolled their eyes

and say it with a drawn out lisp. After she moved to the
west coast in her twenties, men like Hart were scandalous
and exotic to Kim—their unembarrassed exuberance. The
subtle touches of vanity and primping—a bracelet here, an
overgroomed sideburn there, an undone button exposing
a toned, deliberate hint of chest. The deep, sexy joy of it.
The fearlessness.

But the word she could no longer use was *ease*. Not about
Hart. It was a studied ease. Which was not, in fact, ease.

And ease was so much what she wanted; what she
thought she loved.

"WHAT'S MOST UNFAIR," said Kim, about two hours in, "is
I can't even be angry. Being angry makes me a bad person."

"Nothing makes you a bad person," Hart said. "You
have every right to feel your feelings."

Kim gulped back a welling clump of rage. Her father
and brothers were clamouring in her head—clamouring
for Hart's effete, oblivious, hippie-dippy blood. *Feel my feelings? Did you just say that?*

"No I don't," said Kim. "Because you've suffered. You've
suffered things I can't even imagine."

"And I've dealt with it. I've faced my demons."

Did you seriously just say—

But why do I is the question.

Why do I have to face them too?

"Hart," said Kim. "As far as I'm concerned, you have
every right not to get over what happened to you. Not to
speak to him again."

"But that would be wrong," said Hart. "That wouldn't be the right thing to do."

"It's not —"

"Just one second, honey," said Hart. His lips whitened, mashed together in concentration as he negotiated the idiotic car around the latest in what felt to Kim like an endless series of terrifying turns. The road rose and fell and twisted through miles of hilly, outsized forest, and whenever Kim dared to look out her window there was more often than not just a sheer drop into a maw of clustered spruce beneath her.

The road did not even out for a long time. Hart concentrated and Kim forgot what she wanted to say.

After another hour of driving, she remembered.

"It's not a question of right or wrong," she said. "It's a question of what's best for you."

Hart drove in silence with his mouth moving. He was trying to remember where they left off.

"What I mean by *right*," he said at last, "is the same as what you mean by *best*. What's best for me and what's right for me is to not lose touch with my family."

"Is he even a member of your family anymore? I mean after what he's done, does he even have a right to call himself —"

"It's weird how we keep talking about rights," interrupted Hart. "Like it's a legal matter."

Kim could not stop herself from pouncing on this. "Well — *yeah* — that's a whole other —"

"Honey, no," said Hart.

She sat back. He had told her, very firmly, on the ferry

that police had never been an option. That he had chosen "a different path."

"It's not an issue of our *rights*," said Hart, actually laughing a little at the word. "I have every *right* to hate him; he has no *right* to be in my life anymore—to be a part of the family. I said that kind of stuff to myself for years. It didn't resolve anything. It didn't help me to be okay."

It didn't help me to be okay—Kim was starting to recognize Hart's therapy-language. She didn't know if he was trotting it out more than usual, or if he'd always used it and she just hadn't noticed—had thought of it as his own unique vernacular.

They were driving along the ocean now. It was blinding and as big as the sky.

"Everything is too big on this coast," said Kim. "Too much."

THEN THEY JUST did yoga for two straight days.

Everything is stupid here, thought Kim in Downward Dog. She allowed herself to think whatever she wanted as she moved through the postures, didn't censor the worst of herself. Bunch of idiots, she thought in Reverse Warrior, gazing into the mirror at the roomful of knotted bodies of which she was one. Waste of time, she thought in Dancer's Pose. Her family would be appalled to know what she was doing this weekend.

But that was the kind of thing Kim did, after all, her family would have joked to one another—had been joking to themselves for years. Pay good money to stand around on one foot and tell herself she's better off for the experience, healed by all the pointless exertion and suffering. By the live drummer, shirtless and ecstatic in the corner. By the stink of contorted men on every side.

Because Kim was the kind of person who moved to the west coast to go to art school in the most expensive city in the country.

Because Kim was the kind of person who took a job in a copy shop so she could concentrate on music as the years passed and she grew less young. Who lived with a depressed person for eleven years and somehow convinced herself his passivity meant he couldn't live without her. Who deliberately straddled the poverty line, who chose basement apartments of her own free will. Who dated people like herself—people with too many guitars and not enough square footage. As the charm of it trickled away.

And what did she spend her meagre earnings on? What sort of recreations? With what manner of man?

Kim stared at herself in the mirror, balanced in Eagle Pose, a twisted, one-legged malformation.

ON THE SECOND day, something shifted. She felt the clump of rage she'd swallowed in the car nudge its way upward from her stomach, lodge centre-chest and pop like a blister. She sank into Child's Pose and placed her forehead against the mat, losing track of her breathing. The instructor knelt beside her and placed a hand against her sacrum.

"This happens sometimes," he told her, warmth radiating

from his palm. "Everyone else," he called to the room, "please take a vinyasa."

A person couldn't nurse a rage-clump through two days of non-stop yoga, she later understood. The body would not have it. At some point in all the stretching and breathing and releasing the ultimate release had to be undergone.

She felt so much better, felt she had reached a new level; worked through her inbred negativity and come out the other end to take honest stock of the glory that surrounded her. She was lucky; she was blessed. She played music for a living. She was in one of the most beautiful places on earth, eating great food, exercising her body, accompanied by a man unlike any she had ever met—a man who wanted only happiness, who courted it the way other men she'd dated courted the opposite: reflexive pessimism and bogus outrage and—most tedious of all—irony. Hart was the most un-ironic person in the world. He had come through the kind of life that a guy like the Tom Waits imitator from Point Grey, for example, could never comprehend. Hart had experienced enough honest-to-goodness suffering in his life—he didn't indulge the affected kind. He chose light over dark, wellness over addiction, exuberance over cool—he told her that he loved her on the hour.

EVEN AFTER THE eight hours of talking in the car, going over and over everything, Hart never told her what Wilf had done exactly. He wanted to spare her, he said, the "gory details."

"But if I'm going to meet this man," she said. "If you

are expecting me to sit across a table from him, to shake his hand."

"That's why I want to spare you," he said.

"But, Hart, that's not —"

"Two times," said Hart. "Only two. It was not—it was just two times. And both times drugs were involved. Never when he was straight. If it had been ongoing, if it had been systematic—we wouldn't have a relationship right now. It's important to understand my family has been torn apart by substance abuse, honey. I mean even before Wilf—going back to my grandparents and beyond. We're all broken vessels."

Hart told her his father had been clean for seventeen years. What Kim needed to understand was that Hart and Wilf had gone through everything already—confession, counselling, tears, apologies. The "journey," as he called it. But Kim was starting at the beginning, he explained; that's what made it hard for her. It was a journey Kim had just begun to undertake.

She wanted to say, But maybe I haven't yet, though, Hart.

"When we get back home," said Hart, "I would love it if you'd come to counselling with me, honey."

THEY WOULD CAMP at Ucluelet and they would surf and the next day they'd see Wilf.

There was no time for conversation the day of their surfing lesson, an experience that was somehow exhilarating and tedious all at once. When Hart first proposed it, she'd imagined the California stereotype, soaring atop the waves in a bikini, but the water was apparently never warm on this coast, not even at the height of summer. She and Hart were zipped from head to toe in two-inch-thick elephant-skins of neoprene—they even had the option to wear hoods, an option Kim accepted. She pulled it over her head and faced the ocean, feeling weirdly safe, like a swaddled baby must—all tucked in.

"Body condom," exclaimed Hart, pulling out his phone to take a picture.

Once the instructor had taught them the basics, the whole day was paddling out past the breakers and waiting for a wave, then catching the wave and trying to stand up on the board, which Hart achieved immediately and Kim did not do once. But the ride itself was thrilling, even lying flat, and here was another cliché that broke over her with sudden, vivid reality—catching a wave. *Catch a wave, and you're sitting on top of the world.* It was true—it was a rush. Aging, adulthood, it was all about the eventual comprehension that people repeated what seemed like tired bullshit at you over and over again in life until it finally sunk in.

After a while Kim kept getting sloshed off her surfboard. She was trying to get out past the breakers as before, but a swell would always rise up and slosh her into the water, where she'd roll around like a crab before yanking the board back to her with the tether around her ankle and managing to hoist herself up onto it again. She couldn't figure out what was happening, what had changed, until the instructor shouted to her and pointed at the shore. Getting there seemed to take forever. She'd been paddling around in the waves for over two hours, she realized—just mindlessly paddling to get out past the breakers and waiting for a wave, then doing it all over again, countless times, one wave after another. She was exhausted and hadn't known.

THEY MURMURED TO each other in their sleeping bags. Kim almost wished they weren't camping so close to the ocean. After the surfing, all she could see when she closed her eyes were waves rushing forward from the horizon. She could still feel them beneath her, moving, and she braced instinctively as she lay there, engaged her core muscles the way the instructor had taught. The same thing was happening to Hart. As they'd start to doze, the motion of the waves would jerk them awake. On top of all that, there was the sound of the ocean, the actual ocean as opposed to the hallucinatory one, constant in their ears.

"Guh!" said Hart, jerking awake beside her. "Did you feel that?"

Kim started to giggle, punchy with fatigue. "Go to sleep, Hart."

"I'm so tired, and they keep waking me up."

"I know."

"I'm getting seasick."

"I know."

"We didn't even have sex today!" Hart moaned. Then fell asleep with a soft gasp.

They had not had sex that day because there was no time to have sex, there was no time to talk, there had been no time to do anything but surf, and once the surfing was over they were spent.

Addicts are manipulators, she remembered Hart saying about Will.

Drifting off as she dodged the imaginary waves, it occurred to Kim that Hart would have known the effect the yoga retreat would have on her too—he'd been on it himself several times before. The gentle way her knot of rage came loose—he would have predicted it. Hart had taught yoga himself for a while, and Lionel, the instructor at the retreat, was a close, personal friend. Like practically everyone who came into contact with Hart became a close, personal friend.

Hart had been busy keeping her busy this whole time, keeping her loose and flexible, spending all her energy so that there would be nothing left to fuel her outrage and disgust on the day she met his father.

At the yoga retreat, as she crouched with her head against the mat, she had visualized—at the suggestion of Lionel—her heart opening up like a flower. Now she visualized it closing up again.

IN THE MORNING Hart had his guitar out—Kim could just make out "Blackbird" above the surf. Hart once said it was his favourite Beatles song because it took him forever, when he was a teenager, to get the hang of the weird chord progression—so learning it had been a triumph. (Kim had the same experience with "Blackbird" growing up—practically everyone who played guitar did—but she didn't say this to

Hart.) During the retreat, Kim had made Hart hide the guitar in the trunk of the Cube because she couldn't bear the prospect of being cajoled into all-night campfire singalongs with the other yogis. She loved singing with Hart but she hated the kind of songs that normal people liked—the kind where everybody knew the words. That whiny, condescending Cat Stevens song, for example. *I'll always remember you like a child, girl.* People sitting around firepits could never get enough of it. And she didn't like it when people who didn't know how to sing sang. This seemed like madness to Hart, who was always looking for a gig—paid or unpaid—because "you never know who's in the audience, honey." Hart played for anyone, anytime. He prided himself on knowing every campfire favourite and would often say he "hadn't got the job done" if people didn't sing along.

She crawled out of the tent and said, "Can't do it, Hart," when he looked up at her. He pulled the strap over his head and put the guitar aside.

"It won't even be a meal. It's just a couple of hours for tea, honey."

"I can't be in the same room with him."

"He's my dad, honey."

"I mean, it makes me sick, Hart."

Hart caved in like he had a cramp. He just sat like that and it took Kim a few minutes to understand how much she'd hurt his feelings.

SHE SHOOK HIS hand. She sat across the table from him.

His girlfriend was only one year older than Kim.

They drank tea, herbal, and the girlfriend served gluten-free cookies sweetened with agave syrup, which Hart nonetheless declined.

Wilf had clean, shaggy hair, silvery blond, and looked to be in incredible shape for a man his age. He had moved to Ucluelet for the surfing, he told her. He worked as a chef at the resort in Tofino before retiring just a couple of years ago. He had met his girlfriend, Cedar, there, where she still worked, managing the restaurant.

"Do you like storms?" Cedar asked Kim.

"Do I like storms?" Kim repeated.

"Watching storms? The dining room at the inn is the best place to watch storms on the entire coast. You guys should stop in for a drink if the weather takes a turn." Kim wondered if Cedar was being diplomatic about their finances in suggesting they go to the restaurant for a drink and not dinner.

Wilf had all his guitars mounted on one wall of the living room. As his ex-wife had plants, so Wilf had guitars.

Eight hours north, in cougar-stalked Port Alice, Kim had thought that Brenda and Arlo resembled Hart—that they were stunted versions of him, shrunken by their terrible, terrified lives.

But it turned out she had imagined that. Hart resembled his father or no one. When Wilf crossed the room for an embrace, no one's head ended up in anyone's chest—they were precisely the same height, with the same ropey, over-toned limbs. The same shameless rooster's chest.

She went to use the bathroom just as everyone was moving outside onto the patio. Cedar stayed in the kitchen to clear away the cups. The window was open in the bathroom, and Hart and his father stood almost directly beneath it.

"Have a seat," she heard Wilf say to Hart.

Now they are alone together, thought Kim. Now they are going to say something alone together.

But they talked about her instead.

"Nice girl," said Wilf.

"She really is."

"A bit older, eh?"

"A few years."

"What's that like?"

"It's what I need right now," said Hart.

Kim sat holding a wad of tissue in one fist. The fist was in the air, like she was showing it to someone.

"But it's going well?" said Wilf after a moment or two.

"Yes, Wilf. It's going really well. That's why we're here."

"Well, I just worry about you," said Wilf. "I would hate to see you get hurt."

THEY DROVE BACK to the campground after stopping at the grocery store for dinner supplies, and then they had sex in the parking lot, in the Nissan Cube. Then they carried the groceries to their campsite, set everything up to cook, but instead went into the tent and had sex again. After dinner they went for a walk and after twenty minutes Hart pulled her onto the sand.

"Jesus Christ, Hart," said Kim.

He giggled into the waistband of her pants.

At one point during all this, Kim was thinking, What are you trying to make up for?

And she was thinking, He knows what I heard today.

And she was thinking, Distraction.

And at another point she thought, Fine; whatever. Whatever I can get.

Just before they went to sleep, Hart said, "I would like it if you went off the pill."

Kim said, "If something like that ever happened to one of my brothers? They'd kill him. They'd just get a gun and they'd fucking kill him, Hart."

Hart didn't move. Kim had blindsided him, and she was happy. He believed he had wrung this sort of thing—this *attitude*—out of her with healthy activity and sex, sunshine and ocean air. He thought he could cure her and she was showing him he hadn't.

IN THE MORNING, he was up ahead of her again, making coffee. She heard him tuning the guitar and decided to sleep in and make him wait. Eventually he began to sing, and the longer she lay in her sleeping bag, the louder he got. He began dedicating all the songs to her.

Wake up, little Kimmie, wake up!

Soul of a Kimmie was created below!

Kiiiiimieee. You're breakin my heart!

Eventually he flung open the flap of the tent and sat in the opening with his guitar, belting "Dear Prudence."

Dear Prudence! Open up your eyes!

Dear Prudence! See the sunny skies!

She thought: When I open my eyes, I bet you he'll be naked.

Hart was naked. The sun streamed in behind him.

MR. HOPE

MR. HOPE

I remember Mr. Hope from when he brought the boy with an eyeball falling out to be gawked at by our Grade One class. The two of them stood up there side by side, saying nothing for a good while as the life seeped out of us—our childish noise becoming less and less. I don't know about the rest of Grade One but, personally, I had been riding high up until that moment. Earlier that same day, for example, I had discovered I could read inside my head. Everyone else in my class could only read out loud, and not even very well. When the teacher told them: Now read quietly, to yourself, they would start to whisper the words, mouths in motion. Only I knew what she meant. I gasped: *Teacher, look!* And held up the book to my face and said nothing.

I'm saying that up until the moment Mr. Hope strolled into our class with the mangled boy, school had been fine for me. It was exciting. I'd discovered that I was smarter than almost everyone else. I followed instructions better.

I knew what the teacher was talking about—I always caught on. I was good, also, at being obedient. When the teacher left the classroom for whatever reason teachers sometimes left, I didn't go ape like the rest of my class. I just sat there in the chaos, contemplating whether or not I should tell on the others upon the teacher's return, rolling the power around in my mind like a marble in my mouth.

"This is Teddy," grunted Mr. Hope after a long time of standing up there with the boy. Then he let there be even more silence, as we took the newly identified Teddy in and allowed this alien idea to settle over us. The idea that an eye, on a person, could come out.

Mr. Hope was our school's vice-principal. Over the years I have come to know a handful of men like him, but this was my first encounter with such a man. My mind, which I had lately been so proud of, grappled with him; tried to feel its way around him and settle on something— some kind of soft spot—that would allow it to relax.

"Teddy," said Mr. Hope, his voice like a very low horn, "was hit in the eye by a rock."

He was monstrous to me. Not Teddy, whose face my gaze had bounced off once and refused to come back to, but Mr. Hope. Monstrous because he was doing this to us, but also in the way older grown-ups often are to the very young. Mr. Hope's eyes were unspeakably blue. He was shaped something like the letter D. A pot-belly would have been okay. My dad had one of those and it was okay. But Mr. Hope was all belly, all outward thrust. And his skin seemed to hang off his face the way Teddy's eyeball hung from its socket.

"A rock thrown in the schoolyard," said Mr. Hope.

You think I am breaking Mr. Hope's dialogue up for stylistic effect, but this is a pretty accurate rendering of the pace at which he addressed us. He flopped one pronouncement down after another, always pausing to let whatever he'd said just sit there stinking for a moment like a fresh carcass. I'd never experienced someone using silence that way before. People who speak to five-year-olds typically speak fast, never letting there be silence, casting the line again and again in the hopes of hooking their tiny, elusive attention spans.

Here was the crux of my dilemma when I was five years old—here's how the problem presented itself:

Is this a nice man? Or is it a mean man?

"This is what can happen," said Mr. Hope. "If you throw a rock in the schoolyard." He glared around at us, like every child in the room was likely carrying such a rock—in our pockets; our hearts.

You'd think there would have been crying. But I don't remember any crying.

All the people I had encountered in my five years of living had, up to that point, been nice. Men were nice. Women were nice. Some children weren't nice, but children didn't count—who cared about children? School was nice. School was still new; I loved it. Everyone to do with school had immediately become my family in my mind. My pillowy teacher, whom I adored so much I actually prayed to her at night. The principal, who drove a pickup truck (this startled me when I learned of it because I'd thought the principal would be driven to school in a limousine). The librarian, the crossing-guard. The canteen lady and the janitor—who I assumed, for some reason, were married. I packed all these people away in my heart. They would be, I decided, mine.

But whose was Mr. Hope?

He substituted in our class sometimes, over the next couple of years. Some days we'd come to school and our sweet-faced grandma-teachers would be gone, replaced by Mr. Hope with some colourless sweater pulled over his D, the collar of a dress shirt always poking out from underneath. Also corduroy pants that bagged in the seat, where there existed no actual buttocks that I could discern. This was the uniform of Mr. Hope.

He was the only man who ever taught us, and he presided over classes in the same way he introduced us to Teddy. He'd grunt a pronouncement, glare blue fury until he could be sure it had sunk in, then move on to the next tenet of the lesson.

By Grade Three I had arrived at the cautious determination to love him as I did all the other grown-ups in my life. Mr. Hope, I'd decided, was also mine. If only for the sake of consistency.

He always called me Greta. Greta was not my name. Greta was a girl whose name had been in the register on the first day of Grade Two, but who failed to ever materialize in our class. Who is Greta? Everyone wondered. It was a weird name. We were a school of Lisas and Cathys and Heathers where the girls were concerned. So we were instantly curious about her. Greta's name sat there in the register, disembodied, but after the second week our teacher stopped calling for her and we stopped speculating. Then Mr. Hope substituted one day and called her name.

We all jumped, because we'd forgotten about Greta. Our curiosity was rekindled at once   Greta! We'd almost let her disappear! I think I must have jumped more than anyone else, because Mr. Hope pinned me with his terrible eyes.

"Greta?" he said.

"Shelly," I replied. The whole class gulped a breath. I heard the whoosh of it and did the same, understanding why. Because I had contradicted Mr. Hope. I hadn't even given it a second thought, I just opened my mouth and pronounced him wrong.

He was scowling; but he was always scowling, that was his face. He blinked at me once, scowled less, then nodded.

"Greta-Shelly," he said, turning back to the register.

Something happened then. Our relationship, clicking into place.

By Grade Four, I had become enormous. I came back from summer vacation taller than everyone else, boys as well as girls. It angered and disoriented me and I wanted to show them. I wanted to throw my weight around.

I didn't feel like the smartest person in the world anymore—that had gone away. Everyone else in my class knew how to tell time and I couldn't yet. I just wasn't interested. It didn't seem like something I'd ever need. Then one day my teacher, who up until then I had dutifully loved, discovered this. She stopped what she was doing and brought me up to the front of the class and made me face the clock. "You'll learn this now," she said. "Because it's easy. It's just too easy for you not to learn. Right, class?" All the other students watched me for lack of anything else to do. Every time the teacher asked me if I understood, I told her no. "Shelly," she said. "You do so. You do so know the multiples of five." I told her no.

At lunchtime, I would roll into the schoolyard like a tank, kids fleeing in my wake. I was looking for either David Culligan or Andre LaPointe. David Culligan had too many freckles and Andre LaPointe was French. They were natural targets. At the same time, however, I had to be wary of Michael Elleman. Michael Elleman, like almost everyone else, was smaller than me, but he had recently acquired a big friend with white-blond hair named Bernie.

Michael Elleman humiliated me every day with declarations of love. He would pucker his lips, I would bolt, and Michael would give chase. I kicked him in the stomach one recess after he'd managed to corner me in the stairwell, and after that he started showing up, lips still very much puckered, but with his new friend Bernie acting as a kind of romantic enforcer.

So every day, once we were let free from school, my goal was two-pronged: stomp either David Culligan or Andre LaPointe; avoid Michael Elleman and Bernie.

Life had turned itself into war sometime around the end of Grade Three. I sat around hating my older brother much of the time, wondering how I could ever learn to hurt and insult him as effortlessly as he did me. Not long after he entered Grade Six he'd stopped being my friend. He only played with me when he had no boys to play with. When he played with me, he would sit on my head or chase me around with his hockey stick screaming, "Slapshot! Slapshot!" I had no stick to pick up in my own defence. I threw a jar of blackberry jam at him, which exploded onto the walls, floor and drapes. Every night my parents would hear me screaming from the downstairs TV room, "I'll kill you! I'll kill you!"

David Culligan and Andre LaPointe did not complain to the principal or teachers about my terrorizing them because I was a girl. So I was safe in that regard.

Michael Elleman and Bernie remained a concern.

It was my own fault, getting caught. They took advantage of my weakness: the blank-minded zeal that overtook me one recess after I had successfully nabbed, and was preparing to pound, David Culligan. I had him trapped against the chain-link fence. David had tried to lose me in the trees at the edge of the schoolyard but encountered only fence beyond, and now he was done for.

(I always seem to be telling stories about chain-link fences, it occurs to me now. Maybe because they're a thing belonging to the implicit troublemakers of this world: children and prisoners trying to get out; would-be criminals trying to get in.)

I'd landed a single shot to David's stomach that I instantly felt awful about when someone pulled me backwards by the arms—and next thing I knew Michael Elleman was in front of me, mashing his face against mine.

I cried all the way to the school office, and it was Mr. Hope who was waiting there to comfort me.

"Calm down, Greta," he told me in the low horn of his voice.

I was calming down already. The school office was secret and official, a sanctuary of grown-up rules and swift justice. It smelled like typewriter ribbon and coffee that had been boiled to a tarry stain at the bottom of the pot.

Can I break the rules a moment here? I mean even more than I already have? Because I want to say that now, remembering the school office, I concurrently remember something ten years in the future from that day: I come back to this school at the age of twenty to teach a sexual abuse prevention workshop. It's hard because I still don't quite consider myself a legitimate adult, fit to mix with other grown-ups. On my first day of work, I present myself at the office—this same office, with its very same carpet and hunting-lodge colour scheme—take a big breath before announcing to the secretary: "Hi. I'm Shelly? I'm here to teach sexual abuse." But once I'm with the children in the classroom—my old classroom, the classroom where I gawked at a boy with his eyeball hanging out—I relax again. I am back in my element. I could almost slip into my old desk and wait for the cafeteria worker to deliver our milk. I remove the puppet from my sexual abuse prevention kit—a parrot named "Good-Touch Gordie"—and the children flock to me, enchanted. *Awk!* I squawk in my parrot voice. *Good touch! Awk! Awk! Bad touch!* And I point at the relevant places on the body chart. The body on the chart has no sex, is neither boy nor girl.

"I didn't want him to kiss me," I hiccuped at Mr. Hope. "I didn't ask him to. Bernie pinned my arms."

Mr. Hope was sitting beside me on the black leather couch in the main office. The couch frightened and comforted me all at the same time, because that was where you had to sit when you were called to the office for breaking the rules. But it was also where you sat if you were sick and waiting for your mother to come and take you home. And it was where I was sitting now, beside Mr. Hope, who grunted: "Michael and Bernie will be punished."

I think about that now—that grunting pronouncement takes my breath away still. Not: I'll speak to Michael and Bernie, or: Michael and Bernie will be getting a good talking-to, don't you worry. No euphemisms. Just the stark invocation of justice.

Were Mr. Hope and I friends? Suddenly I thought of something weird that had happened in Grade Three. It seemed like decades ago, but it was just the year before, back when I still loved everybody. Something strange had happened that day—something was off. Our grandma-teacher had some kind of crisis, needed to leave for the second half of the morning. Mr. Hope came in looking distracted. We were in the middle of making Easter baskets, cutting out countless pieces of coloured paper into egg shapes—we easily could have been kept busy until lunch. But Mr. Hope made us put our baskets aside, gave us to understand that he had come to class not merely to babysit until the bell, but to impart a very special lesson.

He glared at us until we settled, just as he had done in Grade One, and once all the noise and motion had been driven from the room he blinked and scowled and asked us: What is love, people?

Hands shot up. We could play this game—easy. We were children. We knew all about love.

Mr. Hope called on a few of us. He didn't know anybody's names, so he gave us nicknames.

"You: ponytail."

"Love is when you love your mommy."

"No. That's not what love is, that's something you do with it. Try again. You: eyebrows."

"Love is when you feel your heart —"

"I'm not asking for examples of love. When you say 'love is when this, love is when that,' you people are just giving me examples. Do you know what examples are? Do you understand the difference? If I ask you what is a rock, you don't say: 'A rock is when you throw a rock and hurt somebody.'"

Teddy's face materialized in my mind; his mutilated face. And I remember thinking: *But that's exactly what a rock is. In that particular case.* And next thing I knew the rock was in my chest—in it and on it, making it difficult to breathe because it was becoming clear that there was something in me that was always rising in opposition to Mr. Hope—that I was doomed to disagree with him no matter how much I wanted to appease.

Around the room, children's hands began to droop like unwatered flowers. If we weren't allowed to give examples of love, we were at a loss for how to explain it.

One dim-witted girl in the back of the class had not absorbed the point. She kept her arm erect in the air, straight and certain.

"You: gap-tooth."

"Love is when you hold a puppy."

Mr. Hope slammed his fist against our sweet-faced

grandma-teacher's desk.

"LOVE IS NOT," he bellowed, "WHEN YOU HOLD A PUPPY."

Behind me, I could hear someone's breath hitching rapidly in and out and I tried to shush whoever it was as quietly as I could.

"Where is it?" Mr. Hope demanded to know. "What is it? Think about that, people. You're all so sure about this thing and you can't even answer the question. I'm not asking you *when* is it. A rock is a small round hard thing. Okay, that's not great, but at least it's a start. So what kind of thing is love? Big or little? Hard or soft? Black or white? Or coloured?"

"Red," whispered someone.

"Why?" demanded Mr. Hope, whirling on the child who whispered. "Because hearts are red? Because you colour hearts red on Valentine's Day? Those are hearts, people. Paper hearts. That's all. Representing what? Representing what exactly?"

It was dawning on me that this was the second instance of Mr. Hope doing something to us—something deliberate; deliberately improper.

My hand went up. He hooked me with his eyes and said: "Greta."

"It's big," I told him, knowing it was important to hold his eye.

He loomed closer, moving imperceptibly like a cloud. "It's big? Are you sure?"

"Yes."

"What makes you so sure?"

"Because," I said. "You feel it big."

Mr. Hope backed up a couple of steps and rested his non-existent buttocks against the same desk he'd just hammered with his fist.

"You feel it big," said Mr. Hope. "Okay," he said. "Now we're getting somewhere. So if you feel it big—like Greta says, people—doesn't it follow that we can start by defining love, supposing it exists, as 'something you feel'?"

He turned, picked up a piece of chalk and wrote on the board:

1. Big

2. Something you feel

Waves of relief. Like the group of us children made up a single muscle, a bundle of tendons releasing all at once.

It went on, the strange lesson, until lunchtime. The specifics of the memory get hazy for me after that moment— the moment of tension released—but I do remember working and thinking very hard the whole time. Mr. Hope kept looking to me for answers, like I was his only ally in the room, his teammate. But that's not what I felt like, exactly. There was a fairy tale I'd heard recently—something about a sultan and a storyteller, and the storyteller had to feed the sultan stories to keep him happy and from cutting off heads.

At one point Mr. Hope showed us his white, awful palms and appealed to the class: "What about me? What about me, people? Who in this world is going to love me?"

It froze us. It was a serious question, because we couldn't imagine the answer. I ran to the front of the classroom and wrapped my arms around his D.

Greta, I heard him say from deep inside his stomach.

Now here sat Mr. Hope and me together, side by side on the leather couch. And were we friends? I had hugged his D, but that seemed like centuries ago. Did he remember? Did he remember how I gave him the right answer? That I was the one who calmed him down just when we were starting to seem like a bunch of hopeless kids who wouldn't ever learn?

The bell rang, signalling the end of lunch. "Go back to your class, now, Greta," said Mr. Hope.

I looked up into his eyes. I was getting used to looking into his eyes. Every time I did it, I understood it was the right thing to do, even as it terrified me. It was like rolling up your sleeve to get a needle, or climbing to a great height—courageous. A feat. There were adults who looked you in the eyes and didn't see you. Mr. Hope was not one of those people.

"Go back to your class, now, Greta," he said again.

I went back to my class. Ten minutes into the first period, the low horn sounded over the intercom.

Will Michael Ellemen and Bernie Heany please come to the office.

I looked around. Some of my fellow children were smiling to themselves bloodthirstily.

I waited. I couldn't concentrate on my reading. I turned one page after another and they may as well have been blank.

About thirty minutes later the horn sounded again.

Would Shelly McInnis please come to the office.

Notice: he always knew my name. He knew it perfectly well.

In the office, Michael and Bernie stood before me red-faced, slack-mouthed, puffy-eyed.

"Do you boys have something to say to Shelly?"

In a soul-shattered monotone, and in unison, they recited: "We're sorry, Shelly."

I regarded them. I cocked my head, considering.

"Greta?" prompted Mr. Hope.

Bernie couldn't stand it. Bernie wasn't hamstrung by his passion for me the way Michael was; my arrogance infuriated him. "But she was beating up David!" he wailed.

"Bernie!" said Mr. Hope. Michael dropped his gaze abruptly to the ground as if willing himself unconscious.

"She was punching David Culligan!"

I don't remember the motion of what happened next, the actual activity. I just remember blinking and then absorbing the new tableau: Bernie had been spun around and Mr. Hope was squatting in order to stick his white face into Bernie's red one. Michael and I glanced at each other—allies in panic.

"You are a puke," said Mr. Hope directly into Bernie's face. "Did she hit somebody? Did the little girl hit somebody? Oh no. Ohhhh noooooo!"

Bernie winced—Mr. Hope was shrieking this.

"You chase a girl around, you little puke, you little worm—and you hold her down—you HOLD DOWN a LITTLE GIRL —" (and we knew, by the way he said this, that it was the worst thing of all in his mind, so sickening that it had transformed a hitherto innocent nine-year-old boy into something vile, a thing entirely corrupt—a worm, a puke). "And you have the gall" (this was the first time I'd ever hear the word *gall*) "the sheer gall to try and tell me…"

Mr. Hope could only flail his hands for a moment. Looking back, embroidering the tale from my adult perspective as I have been all along, I'm tempted to say that he was doing everything within his power to keep from uttering the word *fuck*.

"To TATTLE ON HER!" Mr. Hope finished in a baritone eruption.

Bernie's ducts were all open, flowing freely. Tears, snot, spittle. Michael wasn't looking at me anymore. He would never really look at me again.

ONCE YOU GOT the kids talking about their private parts, there was no shutting them up. *Miss McInnis? This one time? I was in the park? With my friend? And this man? He came up to us? And he touched my private part.*

All the stories ended with that sentence—it almost started sounding to me like *They lived happily ever after.* My supervisor had told me not to worry about this kind of yarn unless the kids were actually talking about their family members. The "stranger in the park" was just your garden-variety boogeyman. Once you lay the good touch/bad touch stuff on them, she explained, the kids kind of get into it. They hear it like a fairy tale, like a story they have to learn by heart, and pretty soon they figure out what the most important part of the story is. It's like the car chase in a movie, or the shootout, or the big kiss at the end.

They need to practise it, my supervisor explained. It's a kind of compulsion. Just let them tell it to the parrot.

So I'd lean down and extend my hand, upon which Gordie perched.

Would you like to tell Gordie about the bad touch? I would ask.

And the kids would all nod eagerly, repeating everything verbatim.

Awk! Gordie would exclaim in response. *Was that a bad touch? Or a good touch?*

It was a bad touch, Gordie!

Awk! But how did you know? How could you tell?

Because I just knew! Because I could feel it! Because I . . . trusted my feelings!

This was the real trick to sexual abuse prevention. It wasn't the actual sexual abuse thing—that was easy. If someone puts his hand here, or here, kiddies, it is sex, which you are not supposed to be having. They got that in the first five minutes. What they didn't get was how they were supposed to feel about it. What you had to teach them was that when something seems weird, when you're a kid, you can reject it. You can turn away; you can say no.

I was supposed to lead the kids in a call-and-response at the end of every session to help entrench this idea into their pink, undeveloped psyches: *You have the power! I have the power! You have the power! I have the power!*

Here's the problem with that for me, though—the idea that you can turn away from anything that feels obliquely wrong or unsettling—say *No, thank you* to the weird and walk home. If my memory is at all accurate, that is.

(And I'll tell you something about my memory. It isn't like memory at all. I don't have to reach back. It's all just there. Everything just settles in behind my eyes, accumulating into a giant clot.)

So here is the five-year-old me, obedient in her desk, absorbing the vibrations of the future, the admonitions being shouted in her classroom fifteen years later by her parrot-brandishing self.

The problem for her is that everything seems weird; everything seems wrong. And everything just keeps on seeming weird, and wrong. A little bit at first, and then more, and still more. Starting from day one. Starting with Mr. Hope.

BY GRADE FIVE, Bernie Heany was no longer taller than everyone and neither was I. I was girl-sized, he was boy-sized. We were all starting to balance out, become average. Bernie, I noticed, was now an inexplicable target for teachers—a natural magnet for their anger. It was not that he was "bad," from what I could see. It wasn't that he acted up any more than the other boys. He'd just taken on a sort of invisible status somehow—a mark of Cain.

Around Grade Five is about the time when children begin to intuit each other's status, based mostly on the cues they get from teachers. No one talks about it—some kids just start getting laughed at, while others get followed around. Bernie seemed to be getting laughed at a lot. The other boys had noticed how teachers yearned to yell at Bernie, so they provoked him in class, whispering insults until he turned and shouted at them to fuck off. "Fuck off" was still a dangerous, novel expression in Grade Five—it didn't get unholstered very often. It became a game to get Bernie to yell "Fuck off" and watch what happened to him next.

Just the fact that Bernie was so willing to yell "Fuck off," I realize now, was indicative of his status. He was always alone at recess. He and Michael didn't hang out together anymore. Michael himself had become excellent at some point; was getting 100s on all his tests and winning first place ribbons at track and field. Eventually, I had to admit to myself how badly I wanted his attention. The next thing I had to admit was I had nowhere near the status to get it.

In Grade Seven, we moved from the school near the water to the one by the highway and Mr. Hope moved with us. I remember the shock of seeing him standing wide-legged and cross-armed in the hall of the new school. Shock because at some critical point during the summer I had managed to convince myself that all of childhood was a dream. The dream had started out pretty good until an occasional ogre appeared and then things just got progressively darker and angrier until, finally, I woke up: a real person in the actual world. Now I just had to get on with it, which I was willing to do. But nobody said anything about Mr. Hope following me out of my dreams.

By Grade Seven, I hardly loved anybody—certainly not teachers. Mr. Hope struck me as more physically hideous than ever. There was no way I was hugging his D again. It was not exactly that so much had changed, but that the bad-dream side of childhood had entrenched itself, had calcified. For example, my brother and I were now simply enemies, a relationship that mirrored that of our parents exactly. It wasn't interesting anymore; it wasn't a battle. We couldn't be bothered to physically fight. We just stuck to our own sides of the house and wished each other ill.

Over the summer, I had been obsessed with the possibility of changing my status, of getting what I wanted. What I wanted was Michael Elleman to be in love with me again, but properly, wakefully, now that the stupid dream of childhood was over.

A girl I met on the beach that summer told me what to do. She was, in many ways, a terrible girl. She told me stories. "I saw this movie once," she would begin. "And there was this man. And he started going out at night and looking into people's windows. And there were these girls, having a sleepover together ..." Or, "I was watching TV really, really late one night. Like I got up in the middle of the night and turned it on after everyone was asleep. And there were these two people alone in a room, a boy and a girl. And they were naked!" Or sometimes she had read the story, she told me, in a book that she'd come upon deep in the middle of the woods. Or in a lonely magazine she'd somehow rescued from "the bottom of a dried-up well." As if there were wells in the real world, along with fairies and gingerbread houses.

I found the girl creepy, for reasons I understand now but didn't then. I knew she wouldn't do for a regular friend; that she would have to be a secret friend, a beach friend. I wasn't about to reject her friendship outright, however. I was too fascinated by what she had to say.

I hunted Michael Elleman for a few days that summer,

and once I got him alone I told him my own version of the stories the girl from the beach had told me. He listened, but he still wouldn't meet my eyes. When I finished, he just stood there looking spooked.

By the end of the summer, I knew I had secured Michael's attention. So when I started Grade Seven I was feeling sort of smug and triumphant. But I was still waiting to see what it all would amount to.

In the hallway, I tried to get past Mr. Hope unnoticed. I felt so changed, I was almost convinced he wouldn't recognize me.

"Greta," came the low horn.

The feeling was like a lid being closed above my head.

He was our history teacher now. We had to sit in a classroom with him every other day. Even though it was our first experience of World History, it was clear that Mr. Hope's approach to the subject was by no means standard. Instead of teaching us units on Ancient Egypt and Julius Caesar, his units were called things like: MEGALOMANIACS AND UNDERDOGS—always all-caps, scrawled across the centre of the chalkboard when we arrived—ADULTERER-KINGS: THE BIGGEST WHORE WINS.

Now that childhood was over, it didn't seem right that Mr. Hope was still able to mess with us like this. It had always struck me as wrong, but now it felt distinctly wrong. For one thing, it wasn't happening only once in a while anymore, on a substitute teacher's schedule. It was every other day. Which meant it didn't feel like play; like Mr. Hope just fooling around, experimenting. But maybe it had never been play. Maybe I'd assumed it was play, simply by virtue of being a kid. Grown-ups played with kids, had been my kid-assumption, they didn't bother with them otherwise; didn't enlist them in their grand obsessions or personal schemes.

I decided to try telling my parents about Mr. Hope.

"Mr. Hope," I told them one night, "said 'whore' in class."

"About you?" my brother jeered.

"No," I said. "About all the world leaders."

"All of them?" said my mother.

"Only the really successful ones," I said.

"Hah!" shouted my father around a cud of food. "Well, God bless Mr. Hope."

I decided that maybe the trick was not to be interested in school—that is, to make my lack of interest as clear as possible to all concerned and not be my usual passive self about it. Explicit non-interest. Mr. Hope called on me one day not long after I'd made this decision. I was busy looking at Michael Elleman at the time. Michael was the one thing in the world I did not feel passive toward. And I hadn't acted passive toward him either. My victory with Michael over the summer had made me feel sort of emboldened about life in general.

Michael always knew when I was looking at him, but still he never looked at me. He would brace himself on the edge of his desk and his earlobes would turn red like someone had bit them. I became addicted to this ritual— doing something to Michael with a look; a look not even returned or otherwise acknowledged.

"Greta."

Nobody ever commented on the fact that he called me

Greta. Not even teachers. Nobody thought it was strange, or had a problem with it. I turned away from Michael.

"Cleopatra," I drawled.

It wasn't a completely out-of-the-blue thing to say. We'd covered Cleopatra last week, Mr. Hope explaining that while Cleopatra was an example of an especially successful whore, her reign had come to an end because she wasn't, ultimately, the biggest or the best. She just couldn't sustain it.

But just then Mr. Hope had not been talking about Cleopatra. She'd committed suicide in last week's class. She was dead and buried, taking her glittering empire with her, and history had moved on.

"I beg your pardon, Greta?"

"Cleopatra. That's my answer."

"I haven't asked you a question yet."

"Oh," I said, playing dumb. "Sorry."

The other children tittered edgily at my tone. Explicit non-interest.

Mr. Hope allowed the tittering to continue for a moment or two before silencing every one of us with his response. His response was that he lit up—he actually set himself ablaze—in a terrible grin. All burning eyes, long teeth, recessive gums.

He even clapped his hands together like a child.

"Insubordination!" boomed Mr. Hope. "Right on time, Greta. Congratulations on your garden-variety adolescent rebellion."

He beamed at me. He batted his eyelashes.

"You're welcome," I answered. It was an incoherent answer, upon which Mr. Hope pounced.

"Oh, I'm *welcome*!" said Mr. Hope, his pitch crawling up toward the grotesque octave he'd used on Bernie Heany in Grade Five. "Am I welcome? I'm welcome to all this? He spread his hands, taking in the classroom, the highway outside our window, the squatting town beyond. "Thanks so much, Greta. What largesse. What riches you offer."

The implication being that I was the highway, with its gravel shoulder full of cigarette butts and Styrofoam shreds. I was the squatting town, huddled on either side of the highway, leaning into it offering takeout coffee and a free oil change and 2 litres of no-name cola for only 99 cents. I was it and it was me and we were of a piece — inextricable and indivisible. Forever.

The even worse implication — that I had thrown open my arms. I had made myself so ridiculous as to throw open my arms and say: You're welcome.

In Grade Nine I became pregnant about halfway through the year. I wrote my midterms in a fog of nausea and stupidity-hormones, and did poorly, even in my best subjects. I'd become an idiot — "stunned" was the word my brother used, as in "What areya, stunned?" Because I could no longer, for example, remember the words for things — once I called my toothbrush "the kitchen" and my slippers "foot tunnels" because it was the best I could come up with. One day, at the height of it, sitting in the back seat of the car with my brother one Saturday afternoon on the way to the mall, I forgot his name. I sat there laughing in disbelief as he stared at me. "It's on the tip of my tongue!" I assured him. It didn't matter, because nothing mattered when you were that stupid. I gloried in my new-found imbecility, knowing I was helpless anyway, that no one could blame me for it any more than they could blame me for barfing up my morning egg before it had even travelled halfway down my esophagus.

I should say it was not uncommon to be a pregnant fifteen-year-old in my hometown. Not that it went unremarked upon, but at the same time, the community wasn't exactly rocked.

History, Mr. Hope lectured us in Grade Nine, is about giving up. And learning how even those famed for their unwillingness to give up eventually have giving up thrust upon them. They stockpile gold in the path of giving up. They blockade that path with armies. They soak the path with the blood of those armies. Ozymandias. *Look on my works, ye Mighty, and despair.* History tells us there is no real might. Might is illusory—do we understand the word *illusory*, people? It's transitory. You don't know that word, look it up, I don't have time to define everything for you. Those are the two things might is—illusory and transitory. Might is not right, people, or wrong for that matter. Because might is not real.

Well, I remember thinking with the compost I had left for brains, *that's good, I guess.* All the invading, civilian-killing armies, the kings chopping heads off wives—they didn't really exist. Or they did, but they died. So they might as well not have.

"All that's left is despair. That's the footprint, people. Let that sink in for a while."

We all sat and did. I stared at Mr. Hope's sweater-clad
D and considered that I now had a D all my own. More of
a lower-case d. And I remembered how I learned to print
them both, side by side, in Grade One. Big *D* and little *d*.
Nice and neat. One after the other. Never getting the little
d confused with *b* like the other children, because I was
so smart back then. I always remembered the way the
big and little *D* faced off—they looked inward, toward
one another, never away. That's how you remembered. I
imagined running up to the front of the class like I had as a
child, but instead of wrapping my arms around Mr. Hope I
would just stand there and face him and we'd compare Ds.

"Greta."

I raised my head. I had been gazing down at my d.

"Sleepy, Greta?"

It was a fair question. I had been falling asleep at school
a lot since getting pregnant. Most of my teachers just told
me to go to the office and ask to lie down when they saw
me drooling onto my own shoulder. Mr. Hope, however,
always woke me up. Sometimes he'd snap his fingers in
front of my face. You're not getting off that easy, he would
tell me.

"What if you throw a rock?" I asked then.

And why did I say that? Partly, it was the stupidity
thing, where I just said whatever happened to be floating at the front of my brain, like kitchen instead of toothbrush. What was floating in the front of my brain at that
moment was Grade One. The truth is, the stupidity was
actually more like a sleep-state—that twilight between
sleep and waking; balanced at the very top of the juddering

chain-link fence that separates the dream of childhood from the rest of real life.

So Mr. Hope scowled more than usual, as thrown as I'd ever seen him.

"A rock, Greta? Okay. What if you did?"

"And it hits a guy in the eye and, like, his eyeball pops out."

I didn't mean for the class to crack up the way it did— I had just been trying to make a vague point about consequence. First an eye is in, then it's out—that was all I had been trying to say. Ask Teddy: did the rock, hurled at you by the mighty—the Mighty Rock-Wielder—leave its mark on you or not? Was it illusory? Was it transitory?

Mr. Hope didn't take my point that way, however. He didn't even seem to remember about Teddy, whereas for me, because of the way my memory was, Teddy had never left Mr. Hope's side.

Mr. Hope wanted, he said above the laughter, to see me for a moment in the hallway.

We stood eye to eye, because now we were pretty much the same height. I remembered how important it was to hold his eye, but I couldn't quite remember why I had always believed this. He began slowly, once he could be sure he had my full attention. The man was a born communicator.

"I'm doing you a favour, Greta," he told me. "It's not my way to take people aside when they're acting up in class. You know that. I like to settle things up front."

I stared at him, remembering my Cleopatra humiliation in Grade Seven. He saw me remembering it and knew I wasn't grateful.

"It's sad," he told me after we'd eyeballed one another awhile longer, "To witness a person actually choose to be garbage … to watch her make that decision over time."

For a moment I just gulped air.

"You can't talk to me that way," I whispered.

"I can't?" He looked dramatically around, up and down the hallway, as if for the Gestapo. "And yet I am. And it depresses me, frankly, that no one else has bothered."

The tears I was willing out of my eyes were trickling into my nasal cavity and now I sniffed gigantically to keep them from escaping.

Mr. Hope made a swallow of distaste. "I remember you as a nice girl, Greta," he told me. "You were once a very sweet little girl."

"You think you can do anything," I said. From the depths of my stupidity and dreaming, I was impressed with myself for saying this out loud—it seemed monumental. But Mr. Hope didn't even seem to hear me.

"We were friends, I thought," he said, and folded his arms, almost pouting.

And because my perceptions were a soup that day, because my memory wasn't a memory so much as it was a kind of piling-up of incidents and apprehensions and I had no ability to distinguish here and now as opposed to then and there; because, perhaps, Mr. Hope struck me as not a man but an eternal principle, a planet around which I would revolve forever, my only thought was: *Poor David Culligan against the chain-link fence.*

I'd had no sympathy whatsoever for him back in Grade Three, when I pursued him across the schoolyard. I hadn't given poor David Culligan a second thought until this moment, six years later. David was just a victim, a forgettable casualty.

And standing there with Mr. Hope, I started blushing. A delayed reaction from six years ago, in response to the awkwardness of that moment in the schoolyard, the excruciation of having trapped David Culligan against the fence. All I'd really been focused on up until that point was the chase. I can compare the feeling now (and I could in the hallway, too, standing and blushing in front of Mr. Hope) to a sexual encounter. The same tentative approach, the same self-conscious embarrassment, which you know must simply be pushed through, and overcome, if you're to get anywhere.

I had bounced David against the fence a few times, liking the violent jangle of it. *Ug, ug, ug,* he grunted with each shove, freckled eyelids fluttering.

Then, I remembered, I had hesitated. I'd been shoving him as hard as I could, but David didn't strike me as a boy in mortal terror. Was David, in fact, enjoying himself? Did he think this was playing? I knew the only way to eradicate that possibility was to punch him for real. Hard; in the gut. Where it mattered.

Who's going to love me?

Deep inside my lower-case d, something was turning over; testing the walls. The comprehension that Mr. Hope thought he was being kindly as he stood there pouting at me in the hallway. He thought he was being *benevolent*— that he had never been anything but. Here is what he had always understood our understanding to be: him kind, reaching down, singling me out, because I was so special to him. More special than anyone.

I was his Greta.

My blush drained off. Our Ds faced in. He held my eye, and I held his.

There was a fence, and someone was against it.

ACKNOWLEDGEMENTS

Ongoing gratitude to Melanie Little and Sarah MacLachlan for their kindness, wisdom, and no-nonsense faith. And to the vital, crackling nerve centre of Canadian literature that is House of Anansi.

Thanks also to Mary Schendlinger and Stephen Osborne for helming *Geist* magazine in Vancouver, another such nerve centre on the west coast. *Geist* published two of these stories—"Take This and Eat It" and "The Natural Elements." The editing process was such that I probably should have been paying them, as opposed to the other way around.

Thanks also to Emily Schultz at Joyland.com, for bringing "Clear Skies" to the world wide web, the *Walrus* for publishing "Wireless" and John Metcalf for liking "Dogs in Clothes." And thanks to Ben Sures for acting as technical adviser on "Body Condom."

Thanks always to my agent, Christy Fletcher.

And thanks to Marina Endicott and Rob Appleford for hanging in there with me through the writing of "Mr. Hope."

© ROB APPLEFORD

LYNN COADY is the author of the bestselling novel *The Antagonist*, which was a finalist for the Scotiabank Giller Prize, as well as the novels *Mean Boy*, *Saints of Big Harbour*, and *Strange Heaven* and the short story collection *Play the Monster Blind*. She has been shortlisted for the Governor General's Literary Award and the Stephen Leacock Medal for Humour, and has four times made the *Globe and Mail's* annual list of Top 100 Books. Originally from Cape Breton, she now lives in Edmonton, Alberta, where she is a founding and senior editor of the award-winning magazine *Eighteen Bridges*.